PENGUIN BOOKS

High Banks, Heavy Logs

Nikom Rayawa was born in the ancient Thai capital of Sukhothai in 1944. He received a bachelor's degree in economics from Thammasat University in Bangkok, where, as a student, he helped to found a writer's group and began to write poetry and short stories. After working for a time in a petroleum business and on palm and cocoa plantations, he finally devoted himself to writing. His previous books are *A Monitor Lizard and a Decayed Branch* (Takuad Khab Khobphu) and *Man on a Tree* (Khon bon Tonmai). He is married with two children and lives in Bangkok.

High Banks, Heavy Logs

Nikom Rayawa

English translation by Richard C. Lair

PENGUIN BOOKS

Penguin Books Australia Ltd
487 Maroondah Highway, PO Box 257
Ringwood, Victoria 3134, Australia
Penguin Books Ltd
Harmondsworth, Middlesex, England
Viking Penguin, A Division of Penguin Books USA Inc.
375 Hudson Street, New York, New York 10014, USA
Penguin Books Canada Limited
10 Alcorn Avenue, Toronto, Ontario, Canada M4V 1E4
Penguin Books (N.Z.) Ltd
182–190 Wairau Road, Auckland 10, New Zealand

First published by Penguin Books Australia, 1991
10 9 8 7 6 5 4 3 2
Copyright © Nikom Rayawa, 1991
First published in Thai as *Taling Soong, suung nak*, 1984

Typeset in Perpetua by Midland Typesetters, Maryborough
Printed and bound in Australia by
Australian Print Group, Maryborough, Victoria

National Library of Australia
Cataloguing-in-Publication data:
Nikom Rayawa, 1944–
[Taling sŭng sung nak. English]. High banks, heavy logs.
ISBN 0 14 014727 6.
I Title. II. Title: High banks, heavy logs.
895.9133

For Kanya & Piak

The elephant lifted his front foot to make a step so that the mahout could clamber up to sit on his neck. The elephant was very big and tall. His ears stopped flapping for just a moment as the man swung a leg over his neck. The woman on the porch of the house came down the stairs and stretched up on her toes to hand the mahout a neatly folded cloth and his lunch, wrapped in a banana leaf.

'Could you bring my bush knife, too, Majan?' he called as she turned to go back upstairs. The elephant snapped a branch off the tamarind tree over his head, causing a shower of leaves to fall. When Majan returned with the bush knife, the mahout put it in the sash around his waist and unfolded the cloth, deftly wrapping it around his head into a makeshift turban. Then he urged the elephant forward out of the shade and into the clear morning sunlight. The elephant's feet struck the dew laden grass skirting the edge of the bank overlooking the river. Majan walked in front of them carrying two empty buckets suspended from a bamboo pole over her shoulder. Her hair floated in the strong, cool breeze, and her cheeks were flushed pink. She balanced the carrying pole and went down the path to the garden, disappearing into the glittering light bouncing off the surface of the river.

The elephant lumbered down the narrow gully to the river and waded across to the far side. As soon as the elephant had climbed to the top of the steep bank, the mahout could see the workshop. It was a wooden building, open and light under a tin roof, a very large and old rain tree spreading its branches to shade the front. The mahout directed the elephant to stop under the tree.

'So you've come home again, Kham Ngai?' asked a man carving wood. He laid down his hammer and chisel, staring at the mahout dismounting from the elephant. 'I haven't seen you for ages. Where are you going to drag logs?'

'We'll be dragging right here,' answered Kham Ngai, readjusting the waist of his floppy, beltless trousers to make a more snug fit. He walked past a dirty little boy playing on the ground and sat down on a block of wood by the door.

'Really? Well, you won't have to go into the forest,' the woodcarver said, turning to look at the collecting place for logs. Four hundred yards back from the river there were logs scattered all over a wide meadow surrounded by forest.

'There's a lot. Where will you drag them to?'

'To the edge of the bank.'

The woodcarver looked confused. Kham Ngai added, 'To get ready for the rains. As soon as the river rises, we'll roll them over the bank and tie them into a raft to float downstream.'

'It would be better to send them by truck.'

'It's impossible for trucks to get in here, Boon Ham. Didn't you know that? The bridge across the rapids has collapsed.'

Kham Ngai walked away and pulled out a pile of chains heaped under the workshop. The chains made a soft clinking noise as he pulled them over the ground to hook them to the elephant's dragging harness.

'Where's your helper?' Boon Ham asked. 'Don't you have somebody to tie the chains to the nose holes of the logs?'

Kham Ngai was so absorbed in fixing the chains that he didn't hear. Boon Ham watched quietly for a moment and then picked up his chisel and began to chip away on the block of wood in front of him.

Large blocks of rough-hewn wood were scattered haphazardly all over the carving room where several carvers were busily at work. Some carvings were finished, but many others were only half done. There were beautiful statues of deer, tigers and rabbits. But mostly there were elephants, many only the height of a hand but some as tall as a man's shoulders. The room next door, blocked off by a bamboo screen, was full of stuffed animals. Kham Ngai turned around to look at Boon Ham. 'It looks like you have a lot of work to do.'

'Oh, we can't keep up with it,' Boon Ham replied as he lifted his hammer to strike the chisel. 'Why don't you come and help?'

Kham Ngai glanced over at the taxidermy room. There was a langur swinging from a tree limb, a hawk spreading its wings, and a deer shyly lifting a forefoot. Along the wall there were small groups of snakes, mongooses, civet cats and porcupines. In the far corner a young man was working on a carcass.

'You've already got people helping you.'

'Not enough,' Boon Ham answered. 'The Phaw Liang is pressuring us to work faster all the time. Now he wants us to carve a huge elephant.'

'How big? As big as a real elephant?'

'Bigger. Even bigger than your rosewood elephant.'

'Why does he want it? Does he have a customer?'

'He'll probably just keep it for himself. He wants

to buy the elephant you've been carving, but he can't wait.'

'He said that?'

'Yes. You've been working on it for years. When will it be done?'

'It's almost done. I've set it aside for a while.'

'Well, hurry up and finish so you can sell it. They're getting more popular all the time and prices are good.'

Kham Ngai sat quietly.

'As soon as your statue is finished, please come and help me. The Phaw Liang has already chosen the wood for his elephant. Look over there.' Boon Ham pointed to a massive teak log lying at the edge of the bank.

Kham Ngai looked at it and shook his head in refusal.

'Why not?' Boon Ham cajoled. 'You already know how to carve.'

'Because I don't want to.'

Kham Ngai finished attaching the drag chains to the iron rings at the ends of the rattan breast band and then climbed up onto the elephant's neck. The elephant swung his trunk and let out a loud snort, scaring the dirty little boy who had been staring at him. As the boy ran to hide behind the trunk of the rain tree, Kham Ngai gently nudged the elephant out towards the broad meadow cluttered with logs. The loose chains trailed over the ground, jangling with the swaying rhythm of the elephant's walk. Kham Ngai bobbed up and down as if floating on water.

The elephant stopped when he reached the first log. Kham Ngai got down and pulled the chains to the log and tied them to the nose holes. He climbed back up on the elephant's neck and clucked him forward. The elephant pushed against the foot-wide breast band girdling his chest. As soon as the chains were stretched tight, there was a loud, dull thud as the log rolled over and shifted, the front end gouging a trough in the ground. The elephant lowered his head to concentrate his strength and the breast band dug deeply into the muscles of his chest. He rolled his trunk up into a coil. The blunt ends of his tusks were buried under his skin, and there were deep, slicing scars around the skin covering the embedded tusks. All that could be seen were two white circles, looking as if they had been daubed on his dark and awesome body.

The log rolled with a hollow bang and smashed against the earth, digging a furrow behind the elephant. Grass and fallen branches were crushed, and the earth was turned to powder. Twisting and sliding, the log was pulled over the bumpy meadow to the river bank.

Kham Ngai glanced around, looking for a place to leave the log, craning his neck in an uncertain manner until the elephant finally stopped of his own accord. Kham Ngai shifted his seat slightly.

'It's okay here,' he said as he slid off to untie the chains from the nose holes. Then they turned around to drag another log.

Log followed log. The elephant passed back and forth across the meadow. The surface of the earth was pulverised as every log plowed a track. The elephant's round footprints began to overlap each other. There were piles of green elephant dung where the elephant had strained so hard when pushing that he had defecated involuntarily.

Kham Ngai pumped his feet gently behind the elephant's ears, and the animal arched his back and lunged forward into the harness. Kham Ngai thought of the heavy weight dragging behind them. The log trails began to cross each other randomly. Earth was turned to powder and the morning dew was burned into vapour by the scorching sun. The elephant stood swinging his tail as Kham Ngai dismounted to pull the chains loose from the log and dropped it to the ground with a jarring sound – short, deep and hard.

'One more log and then we'll rest,' he said to himself as they went back for another log to pull to the river. The elephant was walking slower and slower, and Kham Ngai's dark blue farmer's shirt was sopping wet with sweat. He thought of a tub of cool water and the shade under the big rain tree.

'How many logs already?' Boon Ham asked after they had eaten lunch in front of the workshop. 'You're dragging very fast.'

'There's no choice,' Kham Ngai answered. 'We've got to hurry and finish before the water rises.'

'How many logs to go?'

'All of them.'

'That'll take a lot of days.'

'Probably all of two months.'

'In a few days the water will rise, so you don't have enough time. You need another elephant to help.'

'Help how?' Kham Ngai asked. 'There's lots of work to do in the forest. The Phaw Liang won't send another elephant.'

'Can Phlai Sut drag all those logs by himself? His wounds haven't healed yet,' said Boon Ham looking over at the elephant. 'He's really in bad shape.'

The elephant smashed a banana stalk with his front foot and then rolled it up and put it into his mouth. Kham Ngai sat quietly looking at the scarred wounds at the base of the trunk.

'You're right. He's really beaten up,' he said with a sigh.

Kham Ngai remembered Phlai Sut when he still had his brilliant white tusks, thick and long with a beautiful upsweep. But now Phlai Sut's majestic tusks, which had once made him so dignified and so proud, had been cut down to nothing. A few months ago poachers had come and sawn them off.

'They stole everything . . . They left him nothing at all . . .' said the people who crowded to see the elephant the next morning. His face was battered and bruised and he was still groggy from the powerful anaesthetic the poachers had injected. His trunk, normally never still, hung listlessly. The thieves had cut the tusks very close to the skull where they were still covered by skin. The saw blade had cut flesh, leaving horrible wounds and cutting the finger-thick nerve in the tusks. Long strands of congealed blood hung down.

'It's very strange,' said a man who came up close to look. 'The saw cut is very smooth. It wasn't an ordinary saw.'

The elephant declined very rapidly. He showed no interest in food or water, standing still and lifeless all day long. His trunk was limp, his ears were still, and his eyes were glazed and dull. Horseflies swarmed around his trunk, which was becoming abscessed. Kham Ngai boiled an astringent herbal concoction for cleaning the wounds. He covered them with powdered cassumunar vine every day even though he was not being paid to work as a mahout for the Phaw Liang. But because his house was nearby and because he had lived so closely with the elephant ever since childhood, he felt very sympathetic and sad.

'It's like the saw cut your own flesh,' people told Kham Ngai sarcastically.

The aura of majesty had deserted the elephant. His full name was 'Sut Sagna' or 'The Highest Majesty', though everybody simply called him Phlai Sut or 'Tusker Sut'. But after his tusks were stolen, certain people liked to be clever and call him Phlai 'Cut' rather than use his real name.

'We'll get the job done however we can,' Kham Ngai said to Boon Ham before climbing up on Phlai Sut and leaving the shade to drag logs again. 'That's just the way it is, right?'

The thick, rough skin of the elephant flashed in the sun that sparkled in the meadow. The drag chains rattled and the sliding logs thumped along. Up close there was the hissing sound of dirt being crushed to powdery dust. Phlai Sut lowered his head and worked steadily, dragging tree after tree in his quiet and well-behaved manner.

They pulled many logs to the river, where a row of logs began to grow. Kham Ngai pumped his knees to urge Phlai Sut to work his hardest. But gradually the elephant moved slower and slower until he became very sluggish, breathing loudly through his mouth from fatigue.

Kham Ngai released the chains from the log and let the elephant roam free in the cool shade of the rain tree. 'In a minute, we'll do more,' he said, unrolling his headcloth and using it to wipe the sweat from his face.

'Have you hauled twenty logs yet?' Boon Ham asked.

'I don't know.'

'Didn't you count?'

'Why should I count? However many logs there are, that's exactly how many we'll drag,' he said, feeling around in his sash and pulling out the iron head of an elephant hook. The tip of the hook had a point for prodding and a curved four-inch projection off the side for striking or slicing. He gave the head to Boon Ham as if he had just thought of something. 'Can you make me a new handle?'

Boon Ham looked at the dull coloured metal and flipped it around in his hand.

'The handle fell off,' Kham Ngai said.

'You didn't slash at Phlai Cut until it fell off, did you?' asked Boon Ham with a smile.

Kham Ngai laughed. 'You know I wouldn't do that. This is my father's old hook. It's been sitting around for ages.'

Boon Ham stared at the elephant, who was lowering his trunk into a large water jar. 'He looks really run down. How old is he? At least thirty-nine or forty? He looks older than he really is.'

'He's had a hard time. He should be better in a while,' said Kham Ngai, walking over to the elephant. Turning back he shouted, 'Better get a move on with my handle! I'll be back in a bit.'

When he returned the handle was still not ready. Kham Ngai rested until he felt refreshed and then went out to haul more logs. When he came back again and slid off the elephant, Boon Ham held up a piece of teak that he had cut and shaped, though the surface was still very rough.

'It'll be ready tomorrow,' he said.

But at dawn the next morning, Boon Ham was already busy with his own work and had forgotten. As soon as Kham Ngai asked, he pulled the unfinished handle out from a pile of wood. 'Tomorrow – just one more day, okay?'

'Today! I've got nothing to work with.'

'You never use it. What do you want it for?'

'Well, you've got to have a hook with you always.'

'Use the back of your bush knife for a bit,' Boon Ham said, glancing at the two-foot-long-general purpose knife stuck in a wicker sheath at Kham Ngai's waist. 'Phlai Cut always obeys you anyway.'

'There isn't an elephant anywhere that really obeys unless you have a hook with you.'

'You go out and drag for a while. I'll make a beautiful handle for you.'

Kham Ngai headed across the meadow, sweat drenching his body. When he came back to the rain tree, he hurriedly jumped off the elephant's neck.

'You did make it beautiful.' He grabbed the new handle and flicked it back and forth. 'How much do you want for it?'

Boon Ham shook his head and said, 'Come and help carve the big elephant.' He turned his head to the enormous block of teak at the river's edge.

'That's a little too steep a price,' Kham Ngai said with a cheerful laugh.

Phlai Sut snatched a piece of sugar cane in his trunk and stepped out from the shade. They dragged a log and then stopped by the edge of the bank. Kham Ngai released the chains and then climbed up onto the piece of teak that Boon Ham had pointed out. The diameter of the wood was big enough to hide Phlai Sut's back. He examined it all over and thought it was beautiful. The grain was smooth with no cracks or splits. There were no swellings or knots that promised difficult carving.

He looked over the steep bank leading down to the sand bars in the river. They followed each other in long rows like big walls. If anybody was standing in the river bottom, he thought, they would have to tilt their head far back before they could see the top of this bank. On both sides of the river the red earth was loose and crumbly and there were farms as far as the eye could see. The crops were a luxuriant green.

The stairs that people used to go down to the river were hardwood slabs set flush against the earth, almost more like a ladder than real stairs. Not far upstream there was a path for herds of water buffalo to go up and down to drink and to wallow. Their hooves had carved a deep gully like a narrow mountain pass, and when it rained the path was slippery. People would come with their digging hoes to cut steps into the earth, but in only two or three days the water buffalo would wear the steps down to nothing again. Water buffalo do not know how to walk softly. The dust they kick up spreads everywhere. They come in a herd and trot quickly down the bank, their wooden bells tocking, to charge into the water below.

For elephants, going down the steep bank was much harder than coming back up. In order to lower their height and reduce the chances of toppling over, the elephants would stretch their hind legs backwards, walking on their knees. They would extend their front legs, digging them into the earth, and then carefully inch down. The mahout would have to firmly grasp the neck rope until they reached the sand bars at the shore.

In the rainy season it looked very different. Brown and turbid water flowed from the north, rising continuously until in some years the river overflowed the banks and spread to become one with the land. In the rainy season it was difficult to tell that there were steep banks. Some years the banks were eroded in long strips and huge new channels were gouged until houses and trees were swept downstream by the fierce current.

But now the water was very shallow, barely covering the river bottom. There was a long island of clean white sand emerging in the middle of the river. On mornings when thick fog descended, it was impossible to see the river and there would be nothing but pure white. But when the weather was clear one could see vapour drifting in wisps over the surface of the water.

Kham Ngai swept his gaze over the near shore and then looked up towards the far bank. He could see his own house piercing through the green foliage. The house was set on very tall redwood pillars making a high, shaded work area underneath the floor. Not far behind the house there was a knoll covered with grass the greenish-purple colour of fresh betel nut in the cool afternoon light. Kham Ngai let out a big sigh. All around him it was very quiet. He called for Phlai Sut to come to his side at the top of the teak log and then stepped directly onto his neck. He looked towards the workshop where all the men were leaving for home. Kham Ngai rode over and unharnessed the elephant, piling the chains up in the workshop. Then he climbed back up on Phlai Sut and they descended to the river below.

When they reached the water Kham Ngai removed his trousers and used his sash as a loincloth. Phlai Sut sucked water into his trunk and then poured it into his mouth to drink. Then he waved his trunk over his head, spraying water over his back. The sound of his breathing was very hard. The drops of water he had sprayed turned into a thin mist. He bent his front knees and then rolled over on his side to lie on the sandy river bottom, only half of his body immersed. Kham Ngai splashed water over the dry skin of the upper half and then scrubbed it. Phlai Sut's parched, dirty skin turned a rich black, glistening in the sun. The elephant heaved himself over onto his other side to let Kham Ngai scrub the rest of him. His huge ears flapped like sheets of wet cloth as he got up and started to walk to the shore. Kham Ngai ducked under the water several times and quickly scrubbed his hair. Then he waded behind Phlai Sut until they reached the shore. Kham Ngai put his trousers on and climbed up onto Phlai Sut's neck.

Phlai Sut sucked up some water and quickly cast his trunk to the side and back over his neck, letting out a loud snort and shooting a stream of water right into Kham Ngai's face. Kham Ngai was so startled that he nearly fell. He let out a yell and slapped the elephant with the wet and twisted loincloth in his hand. Phlai Sut playfully turned his head away as if trying to escape. He raised his tuskless trunk, spread his ears, lifted his feet and stomped through the water pretending to head for the far shore. Water gushed up around his feet until he finally turned back towards the sand bar and then climbed the bank to home.

'Oh! Is that Phlai Sut?' Majan sat at her loom in the open work area under the house. Her face showed excitement the moment she saw the elephant flap his ears and wander into the shade of the tamarind tree. 'It's strange, isn't it?' she asked. 'He's not sad and quiet any more.'

'Is he like before?' Kham Ngai dismounted and looked up at the elephant.

'Almost,' she said happily, getting up from the loom to stand by his side. Phlai Sut grabbed a whole bunch of bananas and ate them, peels and all.

'The Phaw Liang sent this,' Majan said, pointing to a pile of grass and banana tree stalks. 'He's ordered one of his workers to bring it every day.'

'Even though he hasn't sent anybody to help me attach the chains to the logs.'

'The Phaw Liang said that you shouldn't let the elephant loose to feed.'

In the past, when the day's work was done, the Phaw Liang usually wanted his elephants let loose to find their own food at the edge of the forest. Very early the next morning the mahouts would go and find the wandering elephants, which had been released wearing hobbles and a long length of heavy chain trailing from one front foot. Kham Ngai knew what the Phaw Liang was thinking when he didn't want the elephants set free at night.

'He's afraid somebody will come and steal their tusks,' said Kham Ngai pensively. 'But there's nothing to worry about now.' He looked at the base of Phlai Sut's trunk, where the stumps of the tusks were buried deep inside. He looked down at the earth and then turned away to climb the stairs of the house in a distracted mood. He went to bed soon after eating dinner. Majan stayed up late weaving at her loom. When she finally came upstairs, carrying a kerosene lantern, Kham Ngai was lying down with his eyes open.

'You're not asleep yet?'

'You know, it's good that he doesn't have tusks,' he mumbled, as if he had not heard her question. 'There's nothing to fear, nothing to prevent . . .'

'Prevent what? You're talking about Phlai Sut, aren't you?'

Kham Ngai didn't answer. He lay perfectly still and softly said to himself, 'Tomorrow, I am going to get up at cock crow.'

But Majan was up and about before he was. As Kham Ngai rode the elephant along the edge of the bank, he looked down and saw her on the beach kneeling at a shallow well dug in the filtering sand. She was using a coconut shell ladle to scoop up the clear water and fill the buckets of her shoulder carrier. He and Phlai Sut reached the row of logs on the bank just as the sun was emerging over the knoll behind his house. The carving shop was very quiet because nobody had come yet. As soon as he had hauled the fourth log, people started to appear.

'You're really working hard, the two of you,' Boon Ham said. 'Aren't you tired?' The elephant moved lethargically in the cool breeze, dragging a log behind him almost as if it were part of his body.

'Yes, of course we're tired,' Kham Ngai said, stroking the elephant's ears. 'But we've got to work.' After a moment's pause, he softly whispered to the elephant, as if to an intimate friend, 'We don't have a lot of time.'

Kham Ngai had been very close to Phlai Sut since he was a boy and the elephant was small. They had been born in the same year. Kham Ngai had never imagined that one day he might have to separate from Phlai Sut, but then Phlai Sut was sold.

'If I had been here, it would never have happened,' Kham Ngai said to his friends who dropped by to see him after he returned from two years' compulsory service in the army. Phlai Sut was at work in a nearby forest hauling logs. Kham Ngai stayed home very depressed for two days, until finally he could stand it no more. He missed Phlai Sut so much that he went to look for him.

'Phlai Sut will be back in a few days,' a neighbour said, but Kham Ngai wouldn't stop to listen. There was a long and dusty road cut through the red dirt leading to the forest. As soon as Kham Ngai reached the trees he saw Phlai Sut, tall and looming. The elephant was trying to shift a log, his tusks brilliantly white in the sunlight. On his domed forehead there were thickly caked streaks of dried blood. The mahout on his neck was brandishing a hook in his hand. He was shouting and kicking his feet behind Phlai Sut's ears very vigorously, trying to get the elephant to pull the log. But the log would not budge. The mahout shouted even louder and kicked even harder. The elephant pulled until the chains made a strained, clicking sound. The mahout shouted shrilly and made short, quick slices with the hook. Phlai Sut lowered his head, his ears slapping hard against his neck. Then he lifted his head, opened his mouth and backed up quickly. He roared. The mahout struck with his hook, lifting it high over his head and slashing viciously.

'Stop!' yelled Kham Ngai dashing forward, though he stopped instantly when he realised what he was doing. He turned and ran away as fast as he could.

'Don't think about it. The Phaw Liang has bought Phlai Sut already,' Boon Ham said when he saw Kham Ngai looking very sorrowful. And then, speaking of the sale of the elephant, 'It was necessary. Your father needed the money to get medical treatment.'

'Did it do him any good?'

'You're speaking like a very selfish person.'

Kham Ngai's father had been very ill for some time and had died just a few days before his son returned from the army. Kham Ngai felt very sad and confused. He never thought it would happen. He had always dreamed that he would be a mahout like his father, hiring out dragging logs wherever there was work. His father had been a blacksmith when he was a young man, but then he had bought and raised a baby elephant, Phlai Sut, letting him loose to feed around the house.

When people came and asked his father why he wanted to raise an elephant, he would answer that the calf had no mother and he wanted to take good care of it. The old owner had moved and had been forced to sell the calf.

Phlai Sut was Kham Ngai's best playmate. The two of them would run and chase each other all over the sand bars in the river and were forever competing at scrambling up and down the banks.

'Wherever you see Kham Ngai, you'll see Phlai Sut there, too,' all the villagers said. 'It's like they're one person.'

Kham Ngai would talk to Phlai Sut without a trace of awkwardness. Sometimes he would talk for a long time, until people passing by would shout, 'Does he understand what you're saying?'

Kham Ngai became shy. He would evasively look elsewhere to hide his embarrassment. After a while, whenever he wanted to talk to Phlai Sut he would look around first to make sure there was nobody to overhear.

When he was a boy he loved to watch elephants dragging logs on the far bank of the river, elephants set against an indigo sky. He was excited every time he saw an elephant bend its head and use its tusks to lever a log over the bank into the rising water below. The logs rolled down the bank filling the air with dust and causing the earth to shake. Saplings and grass were shorn off, leaving the earth bare like a shaven head. The logs fell hard, striking the water with huge splashes that rose into the air in white plumes.

Kham Ngai wanted to ride an elephant and lever logs over the bank like that. He tried it with Phlai Sut, getting him to push a banana stalk, but it was not as he had seen.

After Kham Ngai became too old to run and play with the elephant, Phlai Sut was forcibly trained to work at dragging logs and Kham Ngai's father began to work as a mahout for his living. He did well. On the days when Kham Ngai was free from school, he would always ride the elephant with his father. From an early age he worked hard helping his father, whether dragging logs or blacksmithing.

'If his mother was still alive, it wouldn't be so hard as this,' said the old people, loud enough for Kham Ngai to overhear, when they walked by and saw the sweat-covered little boy lifting a heavy hammer to strike a piece of iron on the anvil.

His father and Phlai Sut were hired to do work everywhere. They were willing to do little jobs, everything from dragging poles for building houses to carrying young men on their way to be ordained as monks. When nobody hired them, they would go home and work at the forge. But what they did most was to work for the Phaw Liang, dragging logs in the forest. He offered work dragging logs every year, sometimes even hauling lighter logs all the way to the sawmill. The Phaw Liang naturally had many elephants of his own, but when there was a lot of work he would hire elephants from other people as well.

The Phaw Liang also had a big store in town, which sold stuffed animals and statues carved from local wood. His employees who came from other regions at first always called him 'Mister', but after a while they would invariably call him 'Phaw

Liang', just as did everybody in the neighbourhood.

Phlai Sut grew quickly to be very tall and very big. His tusks were beautifully matched and strikingly white. Kham Ngai's father loved him, but the Phaw Liang did not like him.

'He's stubborn. You can teach him but he won't learn,' the Phaw Liang once said.

'He's not stubborn at all,' Kham Ngai told his father afterwards. 'He's got very good manners.'

One festival day there were tug-of-wars in the middle of a field, with teams of men pulling against an elephant. The spectators laughed approvingly whenever an elephant was pulled backwards over the line. When it was Phlai Sut's turn, he was excited and pulled to the very limit of his strength. He pulled every opposing team over the line until it was no longer any fun. Then, when it was time for the elephants to sit on a stool and lift their trunks, all the other elephants performed beautifully – but Phlai Sut perversely dashed forward and knocked over the stool. Then he resisted the orders being given by people who were standing nearby. He lifted his trunk and trumpeted very loudly, until everybody on the field scattered from fear.

'You made me lose face,' Kham Ngai's father said to the elephant after seeing that the Phaw Liang was unhappy. 'You weren't even willing to sit down on a stool.'

'If it was me, I wouldn't have sat down either,' Kham Ngai told his father as they were eating dinner on the upstairs porch.

'Why not? All the other elephants did it.'

'It doesn't seem right.'

And, truthfully, Phlai Sut was often in a mischievous mood when around people. At one particular ordination parade he had to be decorated from head to tail with a gaudy mess of coloured crepe paper, floral garlands, silk cloth, and patterns drawn on his skin in chalk. There was the sound of cymbals everywhere, and many people, men and women alike, painted their faces, just for the fun of it.

Somebody brought a bucket filled with homemade whisky and set it in front of Phlai Sut, who drank it all. His head nodded and he began swaying side to side, just like all the people around him. After all the young monks had been carried to the temple, Boon Ham lifted a bottle of whisky and poured it into his mouth, dancing about recklessly. He demonstrated to his friends how to get up on an elephant. Phlai Sut, as ordered, grabbed him with his trunk and threw him up on his back. Boon Ham landed perfectly astraddle Phlai Sut's neck. The elephant was feeling frisky, just like the people who had come to watch. He did it again. When it came to the third time nobody was paying particular attention though some people did see a body fly past over the elephant's tail, followed by a crackly thump as Boon Ham landed on a prickly jujube bush.

'It's a good thing he didn't break his neck,' everybody said.

'That bugger Sut is drunk,' Boon Ham told his friends, busily plucking thorns from all over his body.

After leaving school, Kham Ngai often stood in for his father. He never worked at anything else but being a mahout. Many of his friends went to study in town, graduating to become teachers or clerks. Some went to work for companies. Kham Ngai admired his friends when they came home for New Year's celebrations.

'You're looking very foppish – just like a businessman,' Kham Ngai said to a friend who was working as a clerk.

'You could be a businessman, too.' Pointing towards Phlai Sut, who was under the tamarind tree knocking the dirt off grass roots, the friend said, 'What's that? That's your business!'

Everybody laughed uproariously.

But the elephant was everything to Kham Ngai. Phlai Sut put food on the table. And every time

Kham Ngai sat on the elephant's neck he felt safe and secure. So after Phlai Sut was sold, Kham Ngai drifted indecisively. He often felt empty and discouraged.

'What should I do?' he asked himself sadly. 'There's nothing left.'

The vast confidence he always felt on the back of the tall elephant disappeared. He was forced to come down to earth and experience life by himself.

'What should I do for a living?' he asked, sitting talking at the top of the stairs.

'Blacksmith, I guess. You know how to do that,' a friend said.

'Rice farming is better,' said another.

'Do you want to carve wood?' Boon Ham asked.

'I don't know how,' Kham Ngai answered.

'I'll teach you.'

But Kham Ngai didn't want to carve. He wanted to work with elephants. He wanted to be Phlai Sut's mahout.

'He's already got a mahout,' the Phaw Liang said. 'You'd better start looking for some other kind of work.'

Kham Ngai could not decide what to do. He started wandering aimlessly through the village. Some days he would sit for hours sighing at the top of the stairs. Many of his friends grew worried, and they often talked about him.

'He misses Phlai Sut,' Boon Ham said, chatting

with friends bathing in the river.

'He'll forget before too long,' many friends said.

But Kham Ngai didn't forget. Every time he saw a log or an elephant he felt very sad. He was afraid he had dragged his last log, and he did not know what sort of work he could do. He vacillated for a long time, until finally he decided to go and talk to the Phaw Liang.

'Practice for a while and you'll be able to do anything you want,' the Phaw Liang said on the first day Kham Ngai went to work for him.

Kham Ngai worked in the forest doing everything from attaching chains to logs to driving a logging truck. Some years he tied logs into a raft and floated them down to the sawmill, drifting with the heavy logs. He was often away from the village for many days and sometimes for many months.

He got malaria. He became very thin and his eyes sank into his face. He was delirious for many days, but as soon as he had recovered he went straight back to work even though he was still pale and staggered from exhaustion.

Then he was hurt badly when a log rolled over and smashed his foot. He spent many days at a temple recuperating, barely able to stand. His skin turned yellow and his cheekbones stood out. As he was lying there, everything around him was eerily quiet and the silence made him think of the past. Sometimes he idly picked up one of the four or five books that had been gathering dust in the corner of his hut and flicked through the pages. He listened to the wind and the rain on the roof until he felt numb.

Home was far away, at least to walk or to ride on an elephant's back. It would take three days, and in any case, there was no elephant that could be released from work to carry him. So he had to stay in the forest, being treated by the village doctor. He thought a lot about the excruciating pain he had felt when the log had crushed his foot, and he decided he never wanted to work tying chains again.

When the accident happened, he had been bending over tying drag chains through a nose hole. As soon as the log rolled, he had instinctively tried to jump away but he felt his foot being crushed against the ground. He was frightened and contorted in agony. He pushed at the log with all his strength but it was too heavy to move. As he lay writhing on the dirt he heard the faint sound of a drum. He didn't know where it came from, perhaps from the temple nearby. He held his breath, his body trembling and his face covered with sweat, and gritted his teeth against a crescendo of unendurable pain. By the time the mahout came back with his elephant to lift the log off, Kham Ngai had fainted.

That feeling stayed with him for many years.

Whenever he thought of it he would shiver deep inside. It was like the fear and the pain and the sound of the drum were all mixed up together.

The instant he had heard the drum he felt as if he was encountering something inevitable, something he could not avoid. He had to meet it by himself.

Alone in his hut at the temple, Kham Ngai sank into his own thoughts until he did not see the blurred curtain of rain that pelted down. Before his foot healed, he had to spend a long time in convalescence. He moved around his hut by sliding on his buttocks and he had to crawl when he wanted to go downstairs. After a while he cut a bamboo crutch and limped around the grounds of the temple until he could walk normally again. Finally, he was able to return to his home on the Yom River.

Boon Ham hardly recognised Kham Ngai when he saw him walk through the glaring sun to enter the shade of the rain tree. His blue farmer's shirt and floppy trousers were very faded.

'Are you still willing to teach me how to carve?' he asked.

Boon Ham stared at his face for a moment and

said, 'So you're already bored with dragging logs in the forest?'

Kham Ngai just stood there, and when Boon Ham saw that he wasn't going to answer, he handed him a box of tools and pointed to hunks of wood that had been roughly blocked out with a saw. They were scattered around.

'Sit there and get started,' he said.

Kham Ngai became totally involved with his work. He learned quickly. After he had been carving the easy patterns for a while, he started to cut shapes and do whole pieces entirely by himself. His regular job was to carve designs and patterns on tables, chairs and screens.

'I want to carve an elephant,' he said looking at another carver busily working on carvings of many kinds of animals.

'You keep carving patterns,' Boon Ham said. 'We don't have enough screens to sell.'

So he carved patterns, month after month. His hands were always busy and he did not have time for the elephant he wanted to carve. But in his heart he was always thinking that it would not be so difficult. He had done it before.

'When did you ever carve an elephant?'

'When I was a student.'

'What size?'

'Like this.' Kham Ngai held up the palm of his hand.

'Oh,' Boon Ham said, looking the other way in an amused manner. 'You call that an elephant? Only as big as your hand? It's only good enough to put in a household shrine.'

'But it was an elephant.'

'A child's toy. Anybody could do it,' Boon Ham said. 'Anybody who really knows how to carve has got to make a big elephant, at least that big.' He pointed to the statue he was working on. 'It's got to be at least shoulder high, or even over your head.'

Kham Ngai stood listening quietly. He thought back to the time when he had so skilfully carved the elephant at school.

A lot of his friends had simply said, 'It's beautiful.'

Other people asked, 'How did you do it?'

Somebody else teased, 'Did you buy it?'

The teacher had put an arm around Kham Ngai's shoulders and said, 'It's well observed. Don't throw it away. You know, you could easily carve for a living.'

Kham Ngai thought back to what he had felt at that time. His heart raced faster and his face flushed. He turned around to face Boon Ham and hurriedly said, 'Okay, taller than a man. I can do it even bigger than that. As big as a real elephant if you want!'

The other carvers looked at him as if with one

pair of eyes. Kham Ngai turned around red faced and then sat down so he could hide his embarrassment.

People talked about his boasting for days. One afternoon Kham Ngai dropped off some tools at the Phaw Liang's house. The Phaw Liang said, 'So, you're going to carve a big elephant, are you?'

Kham Ngai was silent, and so the Phaw Liang said, 'Whenever you're done, come and sell it to me. I'll give you the cost of two real elephants.'

'Would you give me Phlai Sut instead?' Kham Ngai asked.

The two stared at each other for a long moment.

'Okay,' the Phaw Liang said very clearly. 'And I'll throw in some cash as well.'

As Kham Ngai was walking down the stairs, the Phaw Liang shouted out to his back, 'Bigger than a real elephant!'

Boon Ham heard about this conversation early the next morning and asked Kham Ngai, 'Do you have the wood already?'

'Yes. My father stored a big log in the shed behind my house. It's rosewood.'

'Rosewood – really?'

'Really. And I'm going to make it look just like a real elephant.'

But he did no work on it at all. Much later, after he had married Majan, he could still carve only simple patterns. But when his son was already old enough to run and to talk well, he began to think once more that he would like to carve an elephant.

But by that time the screens were selling well. The Phaw Liang was pushing everybody until Kham Ngai could hardly keep up. Especially after there was an increased demand for stuffed animals, he forgot about everything but work. The Phaw Liang had hired somebody from town to teach Kham Ngai how to stuff and mount animals and before long he was doing a very good job.

'It's a lot easier than carving,' he told Boon Ham. His first job was to mount three hawk carcasses. He prepared their skins and gave them a posture that was very lifelike. They were spreading their wings to land on a branch. Their open beaks were sharp and their graceful necks arched down. He often experimented mounting animals in postures that were slightly different from his standard poses. But when he got well into the job, he would switch them back to the way they had been. The poses he had made first were more beautiful.

'They could be alive,' many of the customers told the salesmen.

A steady stream of carcasses came into the workshop. Hunters from the forest and the local villagers came and sold them all the time. Sometimes friends of the Phaw Liang would come from Bangkok to hunt in the forest. They came in groups of four or five, carrying strange guns and dressed for the part, kicking up dust in a jeep. Each of them would bring a lot of dead animals to the workshop.

'Do a good job for them,' the Phaw Liang would impress upon Kham Ngai. 'They're special customers.'

Kham Ngai was engrossed in his work. Sometimes at dusk he would glance around and there would not be a single carver. They had all gone home, but Kham Ngai was still there. He was never willing to stop in the middle of a job he was absorbed in. He would arrange the arms and legs of a langur with great care until it was gracefully swinging from a branch. If he was not happy with the results he would step back to take a good look and then rearrange it.

He mounted a big deer and a tiny barking deer. Once he did a tiger, trying to give it a majestic and frightening pose, but no matter how many times he rearranged it, it was never frightening. On the contrary, it looked sick and Kham Ngai felt sorry for it.

'It takes time,' he answered when Boon Ham asked him why he was so slow. 'If it's a snake, it's quick – quicker than a mongoose or a rabbit.'

Once or twice a month Kham Ngai would drive a truck full of stuffed animals and carvings to the store in town. Majan worked in the store, though he did not meet her for a while. Then one day as he was strolling through the cool, air-conditioned store he saw a customer come in and say hello to a mannequin standing next to some stuffed animals. As soon as the customer turned around and realised that Kham Ngai had seen his mistake, he was embarrassed and flustered. He pretended to look here and there, and then rushed out the door. Kham Ngai watched him go and then walked over to take a close look at the mannequin.

'It's just like a real human being,' he said with surprise.

'Like who?' Majan asked, smiling at him. She had been standing by the door to receive customers.

Kham Ngai turned to see who had asked the question. He was befuddled for a moment and then smiled.

'Like that man,' Kham Ngai pointed to an employee who was sitting at a desk looking pale and still. 'The dummy is just like him.'

'The dummy's not at all like him,' Majan said playfully and unselfconsciously. 'It's him that's something like the dummy.'

Kham Ngai laughed along with her even though he was not sure that what she had said was funny.

When they met again later, Kham Ngai said that

she had been right. 'The dummy lacked the demeanour of a person because it was a carcass devoid of life.' He tried to explain too much, until he ended up stuttering and abashed. 'But the person was like a dummy because some people resemble corpses in that they have no soul and no emotions.'

She sat and listened quietly, nodding her head in agreement, though with a bewildered expression. Nearly a year after that, when they knew each other better, she told him that she had not understood a word he had said but she had not wanted to ask questions because she was afraid he would feel awkward.

'Whatever you were saying, I didn't get it,' she said. 'But I didn't think about it all that much.'

The two of them laughed.

Even after many years he always liked to talk of that day. He would say he could remember everything about it, from the objects in the store to the clothes that she had worn.

'A short-sleeved blouse and a broadly striped sarong.'

Majan would listen, sitting still but giggling softly. 'I was really confused,' she would say. 'What was my face like?'

'Your complexion was radiant. Green. And red. You were in the middle of a bunch of stuffed animals and your colours matched them.'

Majan said she could remember him as well.

'Your hair was all mussed up and you looked dumbfounded. You hadn't shaved. And your voice trembled.'

'I was shy.'

When he first met her, he told her stories about floating rafts of logs. He told her about a rainstorm which poured down all day once when the raft was caught in a swift current. 'We had to tough it out. There was no way to avoid it.'

Majan especially loved to hear about the time he and Boon Ham took the raft for the Phaw Liang, when they were still very young. The river was so high that year that it covered the banks and there were logs floating everywhere. The two young men fastened the logs into a raft and then floated them down the river.

That trip they had spent twenty days on the Yom River. The raft was very long and had almost a hundred logs. The bow and stern had long sweep oars made of teak secured to upright posts. The oars were called tiger's tails and were normally used only to turn the raft towards or away from the shore. But sometimes the raft would wander an erratic, zigzag course, and it was necessary to constantly steer from the bow or the stern to prevent the raft from turning broadside in the middle of the river. When the raft started to veer, the two of them had to run like crazy, jumping up to grab the oars and row for all they were worth so that the raft would escape the current pushing it to the shore.

They normally travelled by day and rested at night. When dawn broke, if they were truly exhausted they would stay over a full day. The river was very wide. Sometimes there were whirlpools where the water would upwell or suck down as if there were some huge creature rolling his body under the water.

It was hardest and most awkward to control the raft when they wanted to get it to the bank. The two of them would alternate jobs, one man staying on the raft while the other dived into the water and swam ashore carrying a long stake. At one end of the stake there was a length of rope. As soon as the swimmer reached shore, and before the rope was stretched taut, he would hold the stake with both hands and drive it into the earth with all his strength. The man on the raft would wrap the end of the thick rope around a log big enough to serve as a winch. The weight of the raft in the swift current was very heavy. As soon as the rope had been pulled tight, the man on the raft would release some rope from the winch, relieving the tension bit by bit so that the momentum of the raft would be slowed down smoothly.

But most often the man on the shore holding the stake would be jerked back into the water with a splash. He would then have to swim back to the shore and race after the raft and drive the stake in again. If the stake got away from him then the point of the runaway stake would plow the earth, leaving a long trail. The time when total chaos reigned was when a hut or a thorny bush blocked the way. The person running along the shore with the stake would hurl himself into the river to avoid crashing into the obstacle. And then he would have to struggle ashore and drive the stake in yet another time.

The man on the raft had to know just how to release the rope on the winch to control the momentum of the raft with the right rhythm and the right pressure on the winch. He must not allow the rope to rub too hard or to get stuck – too jerky a pressure would be enough to yank the man ashore and send him flying through the air. Sometimes he would be hurled back into the water twenty times before the raft was safely moored to the bank.

Kham Ngai was sometimes tugged into the river time after time for a whole mile before the raft was stopped. When the stake skittered across the earth, he would chase it recklessly, not thinking of anything but stopping the raft. Sometimes as soon as it had stopped he would lie flat on his back, legs stretched out, his lungs gasping for air and his heart pounding. Ears ringing and eyes spinning, he would stare at the currents racing by beside him, seeing it all in a daze.

The two of them were forever inspecting the rattan rope and the wire that held the raft together, repairing anything wrong as soon as they could.

Often the raft would skew around sideways. The men would row to the utmost of their strength until they had forced the raft to straighten out. They would be drenched in sweat as if they had fallen into the water. The logs would twist and bang together until some wire would break. Sometimes one end of the raft would collide with the shore, striking so hard that some logs would get sheared off. Kham Ngai would jump into the river and grab them, paddling with his feet to pull the logs back to be tied up again.

'Suppose the raft breaks apart, and we can't keep all of the logs. Would you give some of them up?' Boon Ham once asked as the raft was riding smoothly on the fast current.

Kham Ngai could only gasp loudly, his body drenched.

Boon Ham added, 'Before we get to the sawmill, there will probably be a lot of logs lost.'

'My body will probably have lost a lot of pieces, too,' Kham Ngai said, staring blankly at the logs as they shifted with the current. 'The raft's too long.'

'If it were only thirty or so logs, that would be about right.'

There was a hut on the raft. Made of bamboo poles and roofed with lalang grass, it was where they slept. They cooked on the shore, gathering vegetables and herbs and firewood there. Fish sometimes jumped onto the raft, most of them flopping into the space between logs where the men could sometimes grab them.

Sleeping on the raft there was always something to wake them up in the middle of the night – the sound of catfish clicking, the gurgling of the current around the raft, the incessant banging of logs smashing together. Sometimes centipedes and scorpions would flee the water and crawl into their blankets. Early one morning Kham Ngai saw a huge snake coiled up in a corner of the hut right near his feet.

'Did it bite me or not?' he said, twisting his arms and legs to see if there were any fang marks. After taking the skin off the snake, they chopped it up and threw it in the cooking pot.

Some days, before they could moor the raft and build a fire, the sun had gone from the sky. They would have to eat in the dark.

'Did you ever hear the story of the grandfather and grandmother who were paddling their boat to the middle of a huge swamp?' Boon Ham asked after dinner as they lay looking up at the stars.

'They saw a big rock like an island and tied their boat up. They carried their little stove ashore and built a fire to cook some food. But as soon as the stove got hot, the island started to shake. The grandfather realised they were standing on a crocodile, not an island.'

'Where did you hear that?'

'Why? You didn't like it?'

'It's not that I didn't like it. It's just that it's scary.'

That night he was not at all happy after he and Boon Ham had carried their blankets ashore to sleep.

'That grandfather would probably never have known, if the crocodile had not moved,' Kham Ngai said softly in the darkness.

'What use is there in knowing that?' Boon Ham asked drowsily, rolling over on the crinkly dry leaves under a bower of bamboo trees.'Save it for when it happens.'

Kham Ngai thought of this story often in the following years. Sometimes he told it to his son and to the boy's friends, always in a loud and happy voice – a crocodile so colossal that it could be mistaken for an island and moored to. After the story was done he would always add, 'Whatever is really big and scary is usually so big that we're not likely to know enough to be afraid until it's too late.'

The water was muddy and turbid, spreading as far as the eye could see. The raft of a hundred logs drifted rapidly and smoothly downstream surrounded by clumps of grass and twigs and leaves wrapped in red froth. Seen from the bank the raft looked tiny. Both men were burned dark by the sun since they never wore any clothes – they had soon learned that the minute they put on clothes they would have to jump into the river.

Kham Ngai stared at the water flowing around the raft. He sat hugging his knees on the central log, his skin glowing in the harsh sun. 'Do you ever think,' he asked, his eyes not moving, 'about what currents are like?'

Boon Ham didn't even turn his head, so Kham Ngai stopped talking. But he didn't stop thinking. Wild ducks quacked overhead. He lifted his head to look at a flock of ducks flying in an arrowhead formation. The birds could probably see the long currents down below. And see me, too, he thought. What is it like to look down from above? Does the water seem swift and dangerous? Now he couldn't see the banks, but in the dry season they could be seen very clearly. The river is just a big and long channel in the earth. The water simply follows that channel and doesn't leave the banks. Sometimes it does spill over to some degree, but it soon returns to follow the old banks.

Fish are the same, he thought. They live in the

channel filled with water. My life is the same, he said to himself. My father always liked to tell me that I was born in a hut on a big rowing boat that wandered looking for hire. Even as I was being born, the boat was drifting downstream. But soon after my birth, my father decided to put down roots and make a living ashore. He wanted to live in a village, and so I grew up in that village. He caught fish in the river and grew vegetables near the shore. He strived for a living along that channel on the earth. So the steep banks are boundaries that work two ways. I live here on this side, he thought, and though I might overflow my borders sometimes, I will always return not long after. But those people who don't return must go to live on the banks of some other river.

And the ducks? He craned his neck and looked up at the sky. There must be banks in the sky just as with rivers. Like the fish. Like me. The ducks seem to be freer – flying in the air all the time to everywhere. But even the flocks of ducks that fly over my house, they always fly the same path. They go over in the morning and come back at dusk. They must have their banks, their own boundaries. But their banks are invisible.

Like right now, he said softly to himself while looking at the surface of the water which spread far to the shore. I don't see my banks. It's strange, isn't it? The water floods and covers everything, but you can't say that there are no banks.

That's a frightening thought. Underwater here there are steep banks many yards deep which are hidden. Banks which cannot be seen. In the dry season people who climb up and down them pant with fatigue. You have to tilt your head back to see the top. I even grow vegetables on the banks. But now that the season has changed, I have floated up to live on the upper boundary. He laughed out loud.

'What's the matter with you?' Boon Ham asked, looking at him, perplexed.

Kham Ngai was still chuckling. He felt as if he were floating continuously. When he turned to look around him, he saw Boon Ham trying to realign the stern of the raft, which had bent out of shape.

'Where are you going?' Kham Ngai asked.

Boon Ham stared at him as if he were a stranger. Both his hands were tightly clenched around the oar, and he stamped his feet several times to get Kham Ngai to attend to the misaligned logs. 'Let's get these damned logs to the sawmill.'

A moment later Boon Ham said, 'You're probably just too tired. Hang on just a bit longer and you'll be able to rest. Don't go crazy just now!'

And then Boon Ham laughed hysterically.

The shadow of the rain tree stretched over into the inside of the workshop. Boon Ham bent his head and struck his chisel into a block of wood. There was a chuckle in his throat.

'So, you haven't forgotten?' Boon Ham asked. They were sitting in the carving room chatting about floating rafts.

'How could I ever forget?' Kham Ngai answered, and the two of them roared with laughter.

'Can you still predict rain?' asked Kham Ngai before walking back to climb on the elephant.

'Why are you asking?'

Kham Ngai thought back to a time they had been on the raft and he had asked Boon Ham what he thought would happen if the water level were to suddenly drop to the river bed.

'Why, our raft would get stuck high and dry, you idiot,' Boon Ham had answered. 'But this water will stay high like this for many days.'

'You're sure?'

'I'm sure. You wait and see – it's going to rain tonight. Don't sleep outside.'

And the rain came. The wind-driven raindrops drenched the hut. The two men had huddled in the shack, their chins shaking against their knees until morning light.

'Guess again whether it's going to rain!' Kham Ngai shouted from the neck of the elephant.

'What sort of rain will we have this winter?'

Boon Ham looked up at the sky while shifting the chisel around in his hand. 'There's only going to be fog.'

'Really?'

'You wait and see tomorrow.'

At dinner time Kham Ngai told Majan, 'There's going to be fog tomorrow.'

'But there's no fog,' Majan said gazing out the window next morning at dawn. It was just beginning to get light and she could see all the way to the opposite shore.

'Where has it gone?' Kham Ngai asked. 'Boon Ham has never been wrong before.'

He and Majan had always liked fog very much. When they first knew each other, Kham Ngai would drive a load of goods through the night, reaching town before dawn. After unloading the carvings and stuffed animals, the two of them would go to the top of a knoll just outside the town to see the sunrise before Kham Ngai drove home.

On the top of the knoll the fog was always very thick. It was as if they had to insert their bodies through the fine particles of moisture in front of their chilled noses.

They would sit down on the grass.

'It's beautiful,' Majan said, breathing deeply. 'It spreads everywhere and when you breathe it tickles your lungs.' Her nose and cheeks were a soft pink colour, and she was hugging her arms and shoulders for warmth.

'Behind my house there's a knoll like this,' he said, 'open to the sky in every direction.'

Rays of sunlight began to pierce the fine droplets of mist. The fog gradually melted away, and then suddenly there was the vibrant arc of a rainbow.

'It's like another world,' she said when Kham Ngai asked her what she was thinking. 'It's like a dream.'

'It's been like this for a long time.'

'But I hardly ever get to see it.'

'That's because you've been in the store too long,' Kham Ngai said. 'Are you ever bored?'

'No,' she said, shaking her head. 'I like being in the store. I don't have to think a lot.'

'It's not at all like stuffing animals or carving.'

'What's different?'

Kham Ngai didn't answer but turned to look in another direction.

'It's difficult, isn't it?' Majan asked. After a moment she added, 'Stuffing animals?'

'For sure. But the more difficult it is, the more I want to do it.'

'And if you couldn't do it?'

He sat quietly with an air of uncertainty. It had been a long time since he had thought of what else he could be doing.

'The stuffed animals you make sell very well,

you know,' she said, to please him when he didn't answer. 'People really like them; they're so natural and lifelike.'

He sat silently.

After a moment she asked, 'Who carves the elephants?'

'A friend carves them.' He stared into the fog. 'I want to do at least one. I'd make it just like a real elephant.'

'You should make it running!' she said playfully. But when she saw him looking sombre, she lowered her voice. 'No, don't. Make it just like a real elephant; that's enough.'

That year the cold season was very long, and a bank of fog covered the knoll every morning. He and she met often but Majan never asked about the elephant statue again. And Kham Ngai never talked of it either, though he still thought about it when he was alone and it was quiet.

After they were married, Majan left the store to go and live with him at his house on the banks of the Yom River. Whenever her old friends from the store in town came to visit, they were surprised when they saw the placid surroundings along both banks of the river. It was nothing at all like the big store in which she had worked.

'How can you live like this?' a friend asked. 'Aren't you ever lonely?'

Majan laughed, her face all fresh and bright.

'Why should I be lonely?'

Her friend stared at her for a second and said, 'I don't understand you at all.'

Majan did have to make many adjustments. At first she missed her life in town and her old friends. But she got used to it, and after she had the baby she almost forgot about everything else. She took very good care of the boy and watched him grow with great satisfaction.

Her son was reaching the stage of being naughty and rambunctious, running up and down the stairs until Majan could hardly keep up with him. Whenever he saw an elephant in front of the house he would shout that he wanted to ride it. One day Kham Ngai cut a stalk from a banana tree, slicing the base to make it curve.

'Here's an elephant. Ride it!' he said.

The boy was confused. After a moment he hesitantly stretched out his hands for it, but then threw it away.

'That's not an elephant,' he said, stamping his feet and crying loudly.

'Why not?' Kham Ngai asked, staring at the boy. 'Aae, take a good look. It's got a tail. What's this?' He picked up the stalk and pointed to a single green leaf at the end.

'I don't want it,' Aae cried.

Kham Ngai lifted his head. The sun poured over the lustrous green leaves. When a breeze came, the trees swayed and their shadows flickered over the ground.

Kham Ngai climbed a coconut palmtree and picked a frond, plucking all the leaves except for two or three at the end. With his knife he cut the base of the frond so that it made a right angle. Then he gave it to his son.

'This is a real elephant. A big one, too!'

The boy stopped crying. He grabbed the palm frond with both hands and then stood astride it, hopping energetically and making happy noises. But two days later he threw it away and yelled that he wanted to ride a real elephant. Kham Ngai got a board and with his chisel carved some legs, making a hobbyhorse elephant. But the boy would not take it.

'What should I do, Aae? Dad doesn't have an elephant,' he said softly. 'Phlai Sut isn't ours any more.'

He picked up Aae to console him, gently stroking his back.

Aae was always excited, running and jumping about. Whenever he saw an elephant walk in front of the house, he would run behind it at a distance, passing the blacksmith's shack, until the elephant disappeared.

'Dad used to be a mahout,' Kham Ngai would tell Aae when he was thinking of the past. 'I had a huge elephant. He was very beautiful. When he ran he would hold his trunk way up in the air.'

Aae asked if he could ride an elephant some time.

'Of course you can,' Kham Ngai said.

'When?'

'I'll tell you.'

Almost every day Aae beseeched Kham Ngai for a ride on an elephant.

'Wait just a little bit,' he would placate him, 'and I'll set it up for you.'

Whenever Kham Ngai got home from the workshop he would invariably go to the shed behind the house and contemplate the huge block of rosewood. His father had collected the log in a year of heavy floods. He had floated the log down from the forests of the north and brought it to shore in front of the house. The river was overflowing the banks so the log could almost be rolled ashore. It took two elephants to drag it over to the side of the blacksmith's shack. Kham Ngai's father had set the rosewood log on beams of redwood and then made a shed of lalang grass to shelter it from the sun and the rain. He had always intended to saw it into big planks to make a table and some screens but he had died before he could do the job.

After Kham Ngai had measured and assessed the size of the log many times, he wanted to carve it into an elephant to exchange for Phlai Sut.

'I know I can make a really big elephant,' he

told Majan who had come in to stand alongside him. He used chalk to sketch in the shape of an elephant from head to tail, making the pose conform to the shape of the wood.

'As big as Phlai Sut, for sure . . .'

'What?' Majan asked loudly.

As soon as she saw that he wasn't going to answer, she asked, 'Why are you going to do it?'

Kham Ngai hesitated. He turned and looked at the wood. Deep inside he felt hurt and disappointed. He missed Phlai Sut so much that he was embarrassed to let anybody know.

'I'll make it for little Aae,' he said, without thinking.

'Are you trying to be funny? If anybody heard that, they would certainly laugh.'

She glanced at the huge log and then turned back to Kham Ngai. 'Little Aae's not interested. He'd play with it for two days and then be bored.'

'I promised him I'd make an elephant.'

'A child as little as that, what does he know?'

'But I promised.'

'He's probably forgotten already.'

'I haven't forgotten.'

Majan spoke with a tremble, her face beginning to redden. 'If anybody came here they'd laugh themselves to death – making a great mountain of an elephant for a child to play with!'

He sat quietly.

'Where in the world are there children interested in wooden elephants?' she muttered.

'I'll make it look like a real elephant,' he
answered with a quiver in his voice. 'It will look
as if it were really alive.'

'How can it? It's only wood.'

'Wood can have life.'

Her face showed that she was unhappy, so he
told her how the Phaw Liang would buy the wood-
en elephant, and at a very good price, too – equal
to two real elephants.

She sat for a moment and then asked, 'How
much do you believe him?'

'The Phaw Liang doesn't lie.'

'Can you carve it?'

Kham Ngai was silent. He let so much time pass
that he didn't dare answer confidently, as he always
had before.

'I feel sorry for the wood,' she said in a softer
voice. 'If you can't carve it, then it will be wasted.
It's a beautiful log. Saw it into boards – there'd
be nearly enough to make a floor for a house.'

Majan saw that he was withdrawn and aloof for
many days. He didn't go into the shed to look at
the log so she assumed that he must have changed
his mind. But all of a sudden one day he bolted
downstairs and went to the shed and began to
prepare his tools. He was soon caught up with
thinking about the rosewood log every morning

from dawn until it was time to go to the workshop. Every afternoon after work he would stay in the shed until dark. Sometimes on his day off he hardly stuck his head out of the shed.

All the time he was thinking that he could carve the elephant. He had felt that way for a long time, though he did not know when the feeling had begun.

'You're only good for talk. You haven't done a thing,' a friend protested.

'Give me some time and I'll do it. You'll see,' he said firmly. 'I have no time.'

'Well, what have you been doing with your time then?'

'Working,' he answered. 'I have to make a living just like you. If I worked only on the elephant, I'd starve.'

Yes, but I'm making excuses for myself, he thought. When I am off quietly by myself, it's as if I am a different person. I can think and I can talk, but I can't really get anything accomplished. Still, even though I'm making excuses, there are good reasons for it. I'm no different from a bird or a fish trying to survive. But there's a lot of untruth mixed up in my thinking too.

Now that he was finally face to face with the huge log he was bewildered and stunned and stupefied. He felt as if he had shrunk. His self-confidence began to crumble. All that he had ever felt so sure about before suddenly had no meaning.

How do I begin? he thought.

He walked in circles around the log, absent-mindedly stretching his hand out to feel the bark, which was flaking off. Many times he picked up his hammer and chisel and then simply stood with them in his hands.

'Strike!' he would tell himself, but his hands wouldn't move. They were paralysed. He didn't know how to start on the huge rosewood log.

Why? he thought with amazed surprise. It's only carving an elephant. Why should it be so confoundedly difficult? There shouldn't be any problem. Other people do it all the time.

He thought of Phlai Sut. He thought of the great fun and closeness they had once shared. He had already asked the Phaw Liang to send him to drag logs with the elephant.

'Absolutely not,' the Phaw Liang had answered. 'You've got great skill as a taxidermist. If you go back to being a mahout, all of that talent will be wasted.'

Kham Ngai felt that he had been Phlai Sut's mahout since birth. He was destined to drag logs. He often thought that if Phlai Sut lived with them, he would be able to take Aae for rides and they'd get off and all three of them would go to bathe in the river.

'We'd run races against Phlai Sut on the sandy

beach,' he'd tell Aae. 'And then we'd soak in the water and you and I would scrub him squeaky clean.'

'When?' Aae asked, as he always did. Kham Ngai could only stammer and prevaricate.

'Be patient. It won't be too long.'

But how to be patient? he thought. I've got to make my own Phlai Sut. I've lived with him since I was a baby and I know him so well. I've got to be able to do it.

Is that true? he asked himself. He began to feel uncertain. Is it true that I know him well? Kham Ngai tried to recall all of the details that he would have to carve on the block of wood. And all he could do was stand there stupidly.

How well do I really know him? Even his legs and trunk – I'm not certain what they look like. As for his toenails, I'm confused as to exactly how many he has. And there's a lot of things far more difficult than that. Kham Ngai thought until his head was spinning.

'How can I do it?' he asked out loud when he was by himself. The proportions of the torso? The length of the tusks? The shape of the trunk? The size of the ears? I used to see them every day, but when I have to recreate them – I just can't think.

It's strange, he thought, considering himself. I've travelled far and I've seen many things, but as for the things that are very near, the things that are most important to me, I just can't see them. It's as if I didn't know them at all.

And the strangest thing is that I haven't known that I do not know.

He tried to start carving the elephant every day, but he could do nothing. At first he had been vigorous and self-assured, unwilling to listen to anybody else's opinion. He had been absorbed and intent. But then he had pushed himself until he had no sense of direction and had become dull and discouraged. Finally, he told all this to Boon Ham.

'You start by practising on that piece there,' said Boon Ham, pointing to a block of wood one foot tall. 'As for the rest of it, we'll talk about that later.'

Kham Ngai followed Boon Ham's advice. He was determined to carve at the workshop whenever he had finished his work stuffing animals. One day Boon Ham leisurely strolled into the taxidermy room to look at the small elephants Kham Ngai was carving for practice.

'You have no sense of process,' he announced.

Many times Kham Ngai thought that he would give up on the big elephant and admit that he was not able to carve it. That was very different from the first day when he thought he would turn the block of rosewood into Phlai Sut.

'It will be done in two years.' That was what he had told Majan the first time she went to the shed to look at the piece of wood.

But after two years he had done nothing at all. The grass roof of the shed had disintegrated and he had been forced to make a new roof. And after that the new walls of bamboo became mildewed to the point where they, too, needed to be replaced – all before he had even struck the chisel into the rosewood for the first time.

His despair made him see another side of himself. When he had been a student he had felt exhilarated when people praised the wooden elephant he had carved. But now any sort of feeling like that had vanished. I get embarrassed even thinking about it, he thought. I mistakenly believed the praise of others and held on to it until I was convinced of it.

One day he stared blankly from the river bank in front of his house as the rays of the declining sun reflected off the surface of the broad river, bouncing into the eyes of the children swimming so joyously.

Those children have never studied how to swim, he thought, but they swim well enough to reach the shore, well enough to jump in and use their endurance and strength to flounder towards the safety of the bank. But their attitude is very earnest, so it looks as if they swim well. In fact, they reach the shore clumsily. They have no technique.

'They can only swim in a tiny little canal or a shallow river,' he said to himself.

That evening he dreamed that he was swimming in a very swift and cold current. He was so exhausted he could barely lift his arms to paddle. His feet, frantically treading water, met only nothingness. He was desperately searching for a place shallow enough to stand. He turned his head in all directions but both banks seemed equally far away. He was right in the middle of the river and growing ever more tired, and he didn't know where to go. All he could do was to try to keep from sinking. He couldn't decide which shore to head for. He would surely sink before he reached land. When he started to choke on the water, he woke with a jerk.

'Aae!' Majan shouted from the river bank. 'Come home!'

She was staring fixedly at the opposite side of the river. Aae was crawling on the shoulder of the bank, pressing himself flat against the ground. As soon as he began stretching out his hand to clap it over the mouth of a hole in the red earth, a kingfisher flew out quickly, its wings rustling. It darted, frightened, down to the river. The image of its iridescent green feathers shining in the sunlight stayed in Aae's mind for many days.

'Why do you want to catch him?' Majan asked

when she saw the boy running up the stairs, his pants still wet from wading across the river. Aae gobbled his food, not even talking to Kham Ngai, and jumped up to go outside again.

'Don't you go to the opposite bank, do you hear me!' Majan ordered. Aae turned around, his feet poised at the top of the stairs.

'I want that bird,' he said, mumbling with a mouth full of food.

She shook her head. 'No, you'll fall into the water.'

The boy's face soured and he looked as if he would burst into tears. As soon as Kham Ngai had finished eating, he took Aae's hand and led him downstairs. He said soothingly, 'There's no need to cry. That bird lives there. You can go and see him another day – he's not going anywhere.'

'But what if he does go?' asked Aae, snuffling.

'He won't. He's got to live in that bank.'

Kham Ngai had seen Aae try to catch the king-fisher before but the bird was always quicker.

Some days, as Kham Ngai stood on the bank looking down at the river, he would see Aae running around in the noonday sun, tripping over furrows in the vegetable bed and falling flat on his face. Kham Ngai thought it was funny. Aae had a way of crawling just like a tiger. Where did he pick that up? Who taught him? Or did it just come naturally? He didn't understand at all. It was like an animal hiding from attack or waiting in ambush – it has known how to do that since the day it was born. It doesn't matter whether it's the hunter or the hunted when it comes to creeping quietly through the grass or lying pressed tight against the earth. Neither wants to be seen, so they use the same approach, like playing hide-and-seek. The animal with the best luck is the one that is the most aware.

'How does it know I'm there?' Aae asked.

'The kingfisher lives in a hole in the ground,' Kham Ngai answered. 'When you crawl on the ground, he can hear you.'

'So how can I catch him?'

'Use a casting net to cover the hole.'

'Can we do it now?'

'No. Sometimes you use a dip net on a bamboo handle many yards long. You slam it down over the hole and when the bird flies out he gets stuck.'

'And if he doesn't come out?'

'Well, then you dig him out.'

'Come on! Let's put a handle on the dip net today.'

Kham Ngai laughed as he walked to the shed with Aae. He examined the log, which he had begun to shape roughly, with shallow cuts in two or three places.

'It's an elephant, isn't it?' Aae asked, his face tilted far back. 'When can I ride it?'

Kham Ngai didn't hear the question. He stared at the bark for a minute and then picked up his tools. He lowered the chisel and shaved off the surface of the wood. He tapped softly, estimating the depth carefully. He concentrated so intently on the mass of the wood that he forgot that Aae was standing behind him.

'It doesn't look at all like an elephant,' Aae said. When Kham Ngai didn't even turn around to look at him, he snuck outside. He went to flip over the boards under the chicken coop, catching the surprised insects with his fingers and putting them in a can. Then he put a fishing pole over his shoulder and went down to the river.

Aae liked to go and look at the people fishing from the shore. He had taught himself how to hold the end of a pin over a candle and bend it to make a fish hook for catching finger-sized mud carp. When he was a little older, he used store-bought fish hooks and he was able to catch bigger fish than that. He knew how to cut a length of bamboo from the clump behind the house, strip the leaves off, and hold it over a flame at the joints. He knew just how to bend bamboo to make a beautiful fishing pole.

Many times Aae had suffered the poisonous barb of a fish spine stuck in his hand until he ran home crying. Majan would rush to comfort him. It happened so often that she could guess what had gone wrong. Still, even though she mumbled and complained, she could not help but jump every time she heard his sobs.

'You must like it if you do it over and over,' she said tugging his outstretched hand to her. There would always be a scratch leading up to a puncture and a trickle of blood. She would wash the wound and smear it with ointment. But as soon as the pain was gone, Aae would forget and go roaming again along the shore in the midday sun.

'Don't you know what it's like to be hot?' she would grumble.

But Aae had always been like that. He liked to sneak up behind a dragonfly perched on a dry branch and slowly stretch his hands out, one hand first, opening his forefinger and thumb and then nipping the dragonfly's tail. If he missed, the dragonfly would flutter away and perch somewhere else. Aae would follow time after time, with his own way of sneaking and reaching out with his hands.

Once he used the same method to grab the tail of a scorpion which was crawling under a bush. When he was stung he was dazed and bewildered. His face twisted with pain. He pressed his throbbing finger for a long moment and then let out a scream.

'Is it good?' Majan asked sarcastically, 'It serves you right.'

He cried for a long time until the purple swelling on his finger had gone.

Kham Ngai made him a lure for dragonflies. He used the fibre from a banana tree to make a line and small pieces of wax the size of a match head in place of a hook. The instant dragonflies saw the bits of wax floating in front of them, they would rush forward, opening their mouths to bite the wax. Once a dragonfly had bitten, it could not spit the wax out, and so it would swoop and wheel through the air just like a fish on the end of a line.

One day Aae walked up over the top of the bank carrying some mud carp strung on rattan cord. He hung the string of fish on the bottom post of the stairs and then leaned his fishing pole against the chicken coop. As he glanced into the coop he saw one chick trembling badly, so he went in and picked it up. The chick just sat in his hands and did not try to run.

'What's wrong with it?' Majan asked.

'I don't know.'

She came to look at the chick as soon as Aae set it down. It was shivering so violently that it could not walk straight.

'Its feathers are all wet. It must be cold,'

Majan said. 'Take it and set it by the fire.'

Aae carefully placed the chick in front of the cooking stove. The warmth gradually dried out the feathers and the chick's legs stopped shaking. It started to cheep and then twisted its head back to preen its feathers.

'It's better already, Mother.' Aae was excited as he cupped the chick in his palms and moved it away from the stove.

At the beginning of the rainy season when the river had risen halfway up the bank, Aae was likely to be gone from the house all day. Most often he would go swimming with all the other children his age. He and his friends would back up seven or eight steps from the edge of the bank and then hurl themselves over, soaring to hit the river with a big splash, the tall plume catching the sun in sparkling white drops. The impact of their little bodies sounded just like falling coconuts hitting the water.

When Aae did not come home to eat, Majan would go out looking for him along the river, because that is where she most often found him – together with a bunch of whooping and shouting children. Their brown skins were naked from head to toe as they jumped off the steep bank into the river.

At one favourite place the bank was very steep and muddy. The children loved to slide down it, their bare buttocks plowing down the incline, leaving long, smooth tracks. If the ground became too dry everybody would take turns carrying water up and sloshing it over the ground to make it slippery. When their flying bodies hit the water they would plunge far below the surface and then pop up to thrash back to shore. Then they would scamper up the bank and get right back in line to slide down again.

One day Aae was bending over getting ready to slide down one more time when Majan grabbed his arm and yanked him out of line. She tugged him along so quickly that his feet hardly touched the ground and his sunburnt arms were stretched tight. Part of him wanted to resist, but the other part was afraid of the stick Majan held in her other hand.

'A lot of fun, huh?' She said, breathing hard. 'Do you think you can just miss your dinner?'

When she heard him start to cry, she shook her stick. 'If there'd been broken glass there, then what would have happened?' She tried to make him understand. 'And there are a lot of thorns, too!'

'That's right.' Kham Ngai nodded his head in a preoccupied way after they had eaten dinner. When he was a boy, he had been exactly the same. He had never thought of broken glass or thorns. He had not been permanently injured. I managed to survive somehow, he thought. Mudsliding is thrilling. Life is like that, full of risks and taking chances. When you're swooping down a mudslide, it's impossible to avoid anything in the way.

'Next time you be careful,' he told Aae. 'Don't play like that.'

Then how should he play? Kham Ngai asked himself. If Aae wants to do something, he'll do it. It's impossible to stop him. If he can't play here, he'll simply go off and play somewhere else just as dangerous.

Is it possible to have fun without taking chances? He thought of his own childhood. When he was a boy he had almost died many times. In the cold season people built bonfires to warm themselves, and when the fires died down they left lovely heaps of fluffy ashes. He had once stepped into a fire pit and waded through the ashes only to discover that the fire underneath had not really died. His legs were burned and became badly infected. He lay in a stupor for many days and his mother had made poultices soaked in fish sauce for many weeks.

And he had been cut by glass, too. It made him shiver to think of it. He had been walking barefoot, even though his father was always telling him he should wear shoes. Somebody selling iced water next to the temple fair had thrown away a glass, which had broken into pieces and scattered along the side of the street. He had stepped straight onto a shard, feeling a piercing sensation in the sole of his foot. When he bent over in the darkness he felt the piece of glass and took it and set it at the base of the wall so that nobody else would step on it. Then he began to feel the pain. When he ran his hand over his foot, his fingers became covered in blood. He walked behind the temple fair and cried loudly. At that moment there was a play being performed on the stage. A battle scene was in progress and the air was full of the sound of drums and excited people. Finally an old man from the north end of the village had heard him and carried him to find his father, blood pouring the whole time. He didn't understand. He knew only that it was a very long night and more frightening than any other night. It was so dark you could not see your hand in front of your face.

Throughout the night neither his mother nor his father had slept. They had sat up with the district doctor, who had pressed his finger against the wound to keep the blood from flowing, though it still kept coming continuously. The wound was open and looked like a baby's mouth. It ran from the middle of his left foot to just under his ankle bone. There was a small basin collecting the blood, and before the bleeding stopped it was daybreak. He lay in a delirium, deathly pale, for a long time. It was many months before he could walk again.

After that he knew enough to put on shoes without his father having to warn him all the time, as he previously had.

'And you've got to wear shoes, too! Don't you

know that?' he warned Aae, who was getting ready
to take his ducklings out to eat earthworms.

Aae had twelve ducklings. He had put duck eggs
under a hen to brood. Once the eggs had hatched,
Aae had tended the ducklings meticulously and they
had grown up very quickly. As soon as he opened
the coop, the ducks would run in a line after Aae
who walked in front dragging a shovel. The ducklings quacked constantly as they toddled along,
their feathers fine and fluffy like cottonwool.
When they spread their tiny wings they looked very
funny.

Aae would lead them to an area by the side of
the house where the dish water was thrown out
from the kitchen. The area was always damp, and
earthworms thrived in the cool dirt. As soon as Aae
put the shovel in the dirt, the ducklings would
surround the blade. When Aae had levered some
dirt up, the ducklings would jab their beaks down
to grab earthworms trying to wriggle away. He dug
continually, smashing the clods of earth until they
crumbled and the worms came squirming out.

Sometimes the ducklings would pull at worms
until a clod actually rolled. But if Aae picked up
the clod, they would ruffle their feathers and
immediately mob together to peck worms from the
ground again. The ducklings always bunched together in a confused mass, never once lifting their
heads. Often one would grab the tip of a worm

just barely emerged from the dirt and then pull it out to its full length – all the while swallowing the worm. Sometimes two ducklings pulled at both ends of a single worm, jerking back and forth as if they were playing tug-of-war until the worm broke and both ducklings fell over onto their backs, their feet pointing to the sky.

Sometimes a duckling would have swallowed almost all of a worm, with just a bit of one end sticking out of its mouth. Then another duckling would grab the worm, pulling it out of the first duckling's mouth and then turning to hide while at the same time swallowing.

People who dig up earthworms to feed ducks are likely to become absorbed in the task. The ducklings scurried about in great confusion and some of Aae's friends would get so excited that they would unintentionally press the sharp edge of the shovel down on a duckling's bill, cutting it off. Sometimes when Aae's friends were wearing shoes, they would accidentally step on a duckling.

Aae dug for worms every day since there were plenty of them. The ducklings' stomachs bulged until they staggered from the load. Some would eat until they were stuffed so full that they collapsed overloaded to the ground.

As soon as the ducklings had eaten their fill, Aae would take them for a swim. The ducklings would waddle along behind him in a disorderly and jolly way. They would swim and dive, bobbing up to preen their droplet-covered feathers. They would stretch their necks and rise partly from the water, flapping their knobby wings. Aae would sit on the bank counting them silently, as he always did.

'If they disappear, you'll know,' his father always told him. 'And you can practise your numbers, too. When you go to school, you'll already know how to count.'

Aae said that when he went to school he would study hard so he would be able to work well and save money. Kham Ngai laughed at the way he talked. Just after Aae had collected the duck eggs, Kham Ngai asked him why he was going to hatch them.

'To raise ducklings,' Aae answered. 'They'll get big and I'll sell them and save my money and buy a pig.'

'Why will you buy a pig?'

'To raise it and sell it. I'll save that money and buy a buffalo.'

'Is that so?'

'And when I've raised the buffalo and sold it – I'm going to buy an elephant!'

One day as Aae watched the swimming ducklings scoop up water and toss it onto their backs, he had a suspicion that something was wrong. There seemed to be fewer ducklings than there should be. He counted again. There was one duckling missing.

He counted quickly one last time and then jumped up and ran wildly back to the worm patch behind the kitchen. He searched everywhere – under the bushes, between the holes in the fence, along the sides of the logs – but he could not find the missing duckling. He turned and looked in every direction, a baffled and frightened expression on his face. After a moment he went to the patch where the soil was all loose and crumbly from his digging. There were footprints where somebody wearing shoes had trampled all over the place, compressing the soft earth until it was like a pit. Aae stuck the shovel in and started to gently lever up dirt, turning it completely. He worked anxiously until he was breathing hard.

And then he found it buried in the earth, its soft and fluffy yellow down soiled with red dirt. He lifted the duckling very gently and held it close to his breast, looking all around, his face very pale. The duckling was soft and its neck hung limply. In its mouth there was an earthworm inching out to its full length. Aae pulled the worm out and then lowered his head to blow air into the duckling's mouth. But it didn't move at all. He blew air again many times. The bird's eyes were closed but the body was still warm. He rushed home and put the duckling in front of the stove to let it be warmed by the fire, and then sat watching over it. His face was sad, his mouth puckered and his eyes red, ready to cry. After sitting quietly for a while, he picked up the duckling in the palm of his hand and repeatedly flexed its wings. He made a little blanket for it, and then put it by the stove again.

'What are you doing?' Kham Ngai had come upstairs and walked over to the stove. Majan set down the clothes she had been mending and came to stand next to Aae.

'It's dead already,' Kham Ngai said when he saw the duckling. 'Why did you bring it in here?'

He walked into the other room to look for a clean shirt. When he came back Aae was still pathetically watching the duckling just as before.

'Get rid of it,' he told Aae as soon as he saw that the boy had not moved. 'It's not going to come back to life. It will start to go rotten soon.'

Aae lifted the duckling in his hands, not turning to look at anyone. With his head lowered, he went downstairs as fast as he could. His hands trembled and he struggled to hold back his sobs.

Majan stared coolly at Kham Ngai. 'Don't you feel anything?' she asked, her voice smooth and even as she watched her son's back disappearing downstairs. 'Aae knows.'

The piece of rosewood had smoothing chisel marks. The shape of the head had been roughed out from a domed forehead sloping down to a long, dangling trunk. The barrel was big and thick like a wall. Kham Ngai was engrossed with it almost every day, though some days he felt blocked up and could not work.

I'm in a bad way, he thought. He felt totally confused, as if he had lost his way, and then remembered a day when he had wandered in circles in the forest until he was exhausted. He almost hadn't made it out. He had no idea of which way to go. Finally he climbed a very tall tree from which he could see the right direction. The first thing you have to know is where you are. Then you can look for a way out, he mumbled to himself in the shed. But the time when I climbed the tree, it was really difficult. I was so frightened and desperate that I started trembling, and I nearly fell from the tree.

Before starting on the wooden elephant, except for the time when Phlai Sut was sold, he had always been full of self-confidence. He didn't want to listen to other people's opinions, even Boon Ham's. He had never imagined that he would encounter obstacles or confusion.

'Hopeless,' said Boon Ham, shaking his head with a very fed-up look on his face. 'People who don't know anything can get along together, but people who don't know that they don't know –

well, they have a hard time talking to each other.'

When he was hard at work carving his elephant, Kham Ngai learned his own limitations. He saw many shortcomings and foibles that he had not been aware of before. So he stopped and considered himself. He was willing to listen to Boon Ham's advice on carving, but when he lowered his hand to work, something stopped him.

'Is something wrong?' Majan was worried. After calling him to come and eat many times, she went to the shed and saw him lying face up on the top of the log, with the back of his hand on his forehead.

'Aren't you hungry?'

'I'm not hungry. I'll get something for myself later,' he said softly.

In a moment he came out of the shed. He looked into the chicken coop and walked past the pig sty to skirt the edge of the bank, not at all interested in the clear and open space around him. Walking past the vegetable garden he stumbled over a lump of dirt at the edge of the water. A stray dog that had been lying at the side of the path jumped up and scampered away.

The dog turned back and looked at Kham Ngai for a moment, and then wagged his tail and followed him. Kham Ngai had seen him hanging around for a long time. Other dogs had bitten him until his ears were torn and his red fur was covered with scars from teeth and claws. One day an angry housewife, tired of the dog's antics, had thrown boiling cooking water at him from her upstairs porch. Kham Ngai had been on his way to work and had seen the dog writhe, twisting his head to bite at the heat. The boiling water had caused a terrible wound and the dog still had a large open sore on his back.

Aae didn't like to be anywhere near the dog. He would cry out with fear whenever he saw him – the dog was ugly. Even though when the dog wagged his tail and the look in his eyes showed that he was tame, Aae didn't care. Sometimes he would chase him away.

'What are you afraid of?' Kham Ngai asked.

'I'm afraid of his sores. His skin has peeled off and his ears are torn.'

Kham Ngai walked slowly. The dog trotted along in front, leading the way, its sore glistening in the sunlight. The dog's nature was very cheerful and quizzical.

'Tell me something!' Kham Ngai said loudly. The dog stopped, spun around and wagged its tail, and then turned around to run. Kham Ngai saw him flex his legs and leap into the water to sprint along the shore. Kham Ngai dawdled behind for a bit and then started to trot the same way as the dog – jumping over a clump of lemongrass, hitting the edge of the shore, kicking up water, splashing all over. The dog ran with his ears perked. Kham Ngai laughed deeply, louder and louder all the time until he could laugh no harder. He changed from a trot and began to run at full speed as if it were a race. The two of them constantly changed places, one in front and then the other, until they had run all around the beach.

Kham Ngai was breathing very hard. He slowed down and then he stood still. When he sat on the gravel at the shore, the dog came and circled around him, putting his head down to sniff the ground. The dog suddenly lifted his head, his ears held high, and crept up to the clump of lemongrass.

'He's got a beautiful manner,' he said as his eyes followed the dog.

A black cat was hiding in the shade. The dog crept along, pressed close to the ground. The cat began to hiss. After a single bark which resonated along the walls of the river bank, the dog lunged after the cat, which turned and ran away.

'Go!' Kham Ngai shouted, jumping up to see better. 'Catch it!'

After being engrossed with the elephant in the shed to the point of feeling dull and morose, Kham Ngai had started coming to the river some days. The long sandy beach was clean, and the air was cool in the broad, open river bottom. He began to come more and more often until he was coming almost every day. Early every morning at the same time a flock of wild ducks would pass overhead. Kham Ngai would trot along the beach, breathing hoarsely to the rhythm of his feet while the dog with the sore back ran by his side. Sometimes the dog would run ahead and then stop, lowering his nose to explore the bushes and grass. Many times Kham Ngai forgot about going to the workshop.

'It's late already. Aren't you going to work today?' Majan asked, putting her head around the door of the shed. He was sharpening a chisel.

These days Majan hardly ever came to the shed. Kham Ngai was always at work, obsessed with his carving. Sometimes he would not look up even when she was standing close enough to touch his face. His eyes never left the piece of wood he was carving. When she called him, the only response was a soft sound in his throat. Majan felt far away from him all the time.

One night as they were lying in the dark, Majan told him that he had changed a great deal.

'Is that so? How have I changed?'

'You're not like before.'

'Not like since when?'

'Since you started going to the shed.'

He lay quietly. Then she said, 'And the longer it goes on, the stranger you get.'

When Kham Ngai remained silent, Majan continued, 'Some days I see you sitting as still as a dummy. I go in to say hello and you don't even answer.'

'You're thinking too much,' he said. 'I'm just as I always was.'

'No, you're not. You're a whole different person. I can hardly remember what you were like then.'

When she walked by the shed she sometimes heard him mumbling to himself. Sometimes he would say only two or three words and stop, but other times he would talk for a long time, as if he were speaking to another person.

Some days he would be so engrossed in the rosewood texture that he would forget to go to work. Before he realised, it was afternoon. Boon Ham asked him, 'Have you been sick?' Kham Ngai only shook his head, and rushed off to the taxidermy room.

He became even more immersed in carving the elephant and missed going to work many days.

One morning he looked into the taxidermy room

and saw many newly finished stuffed animals all in a row.

'Did you do them?' he asked Boon Ham. 'Thanks very much.'

'It's nothing,' Boon Ham said. 'It's all right so long as it's not too often.'

But then he missed more work. He did not show up for nearly a month.

'It's a good thing that there's not a lot of work now,' Boon Ham told Kham Ngai when he met him in front of the workshop. 'There haven't been any animals delivered. But if it wasn't for that, there'd be big problems.'

It was not surprising that there were no carcasses delivered that month. Police and forestry officials had launched a crackdown on illegal logging and hunting all over Phrae and Chiang Mai provinces. They had come often to inspect the workshop. Phlai Sut had been dragging newly felled trees in the forest when he was confiscated by officials. He was kept chained up behind the jail at the district headquarters, and the Phaw Liang had to do a lot of running around before the elephant was released. Both the carving work and the taxidermy had slowed down, but before very long there was as much work as there had ever been.

'You can take my place,' Kham Ngai said.

'I don't have time,' Boon Ham said. 'I can't keep up with my own work.'

'Then hire somebody.'

'The Phaw Liang is looking for workers in Chiang Mai. He's probably hired one or two people already.'

'Did he say anything about me?'

'Well, he complained. If he can find somebody else, he'll get rid of you for sure. He thinks you take advantage of him.'

'I don't take advantage of him. He pays by the piece. If I do the work, I get paid. If I don't work, I don't get paid.'

'But it still spoils his planning.'

The Phaw Liang hired one taxidermist and one carver of screens. They had not worked even two months when they quit.

'Young people are like that,' Boon Ham said.

The Phaw Liang hired some new people, older than the ones that had quit. Without a hint of condescension, the Phaw Liang told them on their first day that he would like them to stay and work for a long time. But they left at the end of three months.

'It's lonely here,' Boon Ham said. 'People from other places can't stand it.'

Kham Ngai promised to go to the workshop every day, just as he had before. In the mornings, when he worked on his elephant he felt very apprehensive, as if he was not allocating his time properly. He was likely to get so caught up with the elephant that he would forget to go to work.

'If you've got any fresh carcasses, send one of the children to my house to tell me,' he told Boon Ham. 'I'll come over right away.'

One day Boon Ham noticed Kham Ngai in the taxidermy room, sitting and staring blankly, all wrapped up in his thoughts.

'Is something wrong?' Boon Ham asked sceptically. Kham Ngai was startled but didn't answer. He only smiled and went back to his work.

'If there's any way I can help you,' Boon Ham tried to be supportive, 'please tell me.'

'What's that?' Kham Ngai was confused.

A week later, after thinking about it for a long time, Boon Ham went back to him. 'Listen, you're old already,' he said. 'If you had ordained as a monk, you'd be an abbot by now. Get to work. You're not a child anymore.'

Kham Ngai didn't understand. He didn't know whether Boon Ham was criticising the fact that he had missed a lot of days of work or whether Boon Ham was talking about his whole life.

Beams of afternoon light thrust into the shed. Kham Ngai struck the chisel with all his strength to slice off a hard, protruding knot from the rosewood. He had come a long way with the elephant. The shape and the proportions were beautiful. All that was left to do was the smoothing and to finish some of the minor details. The ends of the feet and the base had not yet been carved but were still lumps of bumpy, gnarled wood.

He did the finishing work carefully. While working he found imperfections all the time. 'Why didn't I see that yesterday?' he asked himself. 'I wonder if I'll find something else wrong tomorrow.'

Some days he would soothe himself by saying, 'Today it will be as good as it can ever be.' But the next morning he would find something else that needed correcting. He found little flaws so often that he became discouraged. 'When will all of the corrections be done?' he grumbled to himself. 'Will I have to keep refining it until the day I die?'

He buried himself in the shed more and more until his soul entered into the wooden elephant. He didn't care whether it was day or night. Many evenings he would light an oil lantern and work through the middle of the night. Sometimes he worked with complete understanding, the hammer and chisel moving as if of their own volition. But at other times he felt he had no strength for carving.

'The elephant is born from itself,' he said, looking at the parts that had already been carved. 'It has emerged by itself, little by little.'

He was so wrapped up in his work that he didn't want to stop. Time went by very fast. If I had more time it would be good, he thought. I could work more smoothly. It would also be good if I didn't have to stop to eat or to sleep.

He did the fine carving on the ears, which had to be very thin, with great caution.

It's almost done, he thought, as he stood scrutinising the wooden elephant. If I didn't have to go to stuff animals then I could carve all the time. My time would be my own. How would the work go then? I wonder what Boon Ham would say if he saw the elephant. I've no idea, and it wouldn't matter anyway. It's taken such a long time to reach this day that I'm not excited about anything any more.

Was it finished or not? he would think, backing up to look at it from a distance. It's still missing something. What would people say if I told them what I have put into the elephant? I have put in many years of time. I have put in willpower and endurance. There's joy and suffering and fear and courage – and many other things all mixed up together in there.

The elephant was posed striding forward. The dangling trunk was slightly curled and looked soft and pliable. The delicate ears were poised to flap. The long tail looked as if it was swinging quickly, lashing out at swarming insects. Strong legs supported a massive body. It was as big as a full grown elephant.

How many years already? he thought. I've been in here for a long time. He could remember when he had first prepared his hammer and chisel and brought them to the shed. Aae was still playing with toy elephants. But now he has grown a lot – he's running up and down the river bank and going fishing every day.

From that first day until now, the carving had brought him a great sense of relief, as if he had expunged something from his heart. As for the rosewood elephant in the shed, it did not matter whether people liked it or not. It was there. It had its own meaning. He had never once thought of the elephant as having any meaning before. He only felt that it was something he was destined to do. He had never felt that it was a burden or an obligation that had compelled him to pick up his chisel.

There were some feelings hidden quietly in his heart. He thought of Phlai Sut, but it was the mood of a moment. The carving had nothing to do with anybody – not the Phaw Liang, not Majan, not Aae. Until today the elephant was only itself. It was only a symbol that told of a path which had led to itself, a path that he had been following for so long that his black hair had become sprinkled with grey.

Kham Ngai stood for a long time staring at the wooden elephant. He had not heard Majan calling him to dinner, so she came downstairs to fetch him.

'Are you going to stare at it until you're full, instead of eating?' Her voice showed her concern. 'It doesn't matter. As soon as it's done, somebody else will come and take it away. It won't be ours any more.'

Kham Ngai turned and smiled at her. He didn't say a word, but in his heart a new feeling arose.

Whatever happened to the elephant, no matter how many times it was bought or sold, nobody could truly take it away. Every minute of being in the shed, from the first strike of the chisel to the last, that time was something apart and that time was the real elephant. The totality of the experience came back to him with great clarity.

Everybody has their own elephant. If it's theirs, then it's theirs alone. Everybody must do their own carving. There's no switching.

'I'm going to look for a pair of beautiful marbles to make some eyes for him,' Kham Ngai said as they were eating dinner outside on the porch. After dinner, Majan and Aae were very surprised when he invited them to walk over to the shed. They had become

so accustomed to the elephant's slow progress, and to Kham Ngai's taciturn mood when he was in the shed, that they never gave a thought to it.

Before now the shed had always been littered with wood shavings and sawdust, all mixed up with small and large chunks of wood. But today the heaps of scraps had all been taken away and the floor had been swept perfectly clean. The elephant stood clearly alone.

'Is it like a real elephant?' he asked Aae.

Aae was at his side craning his neck to look up at the elephant.

'It's the same,' Aae nodded, excited.

'It's not finished,' Aae said staring at the elephant's feet, which were still lumps of rough wood, as if the legs had sunk into a log and fused with it.

'I'll do them later.'

'There's no tusks,' Aae said, looking up at the empty sockets at the base of the trunk.

'I'll do them tomorrow,' Kham Ngai said. 'I'll use redwood and paint them dazzling white.'

'Put in real tusks!'

'I don't have any real tusks.'

Aae walked all around the elephant, stroking the legs and trunk. He turned to look at Kham Ngai shyly. 'Can I ride it?'

'Sure.'

Kham Ngai held Aae up as far as his arms could

reach. Aae stuck his arms out and grabbed the elephant's neck and then clambered up to sit astride it. His face was beaming as he sat on the hard, rounded body. He looked all around while stroking the ears and the prominent bumps on the elephant's forehead. Gradually he lost his feeling of awe and began to relax, swaying back and forth and laughing. He shouted and prodded with his feet, just like a real mahout making an elephant move. Then he turned and looked down at Kham Ngai.

'It won't go,' he said. 'I need a hook before it will obey.'

Majan and Kham Ngai laughed. 'I'll make you one,' Kham Ngai said, raising his hands to help the boy down.

'It's hard to get up there,' Aae said when his feet hit the floor.

'So, I'll make a ladder.'

Aae took his eyes away from the elephant and turned to Kham Ngai. 'Will it run away?'

'I'll get some chains to tether it.'

'Tether it to what? There's no post.' Aae looked around the shed.

'I'll make a tethering post, too.'

When they got back to the house, Majan asked Aae, 'Did you like it?'

'It was fun.'

'Just like a real elephant, right?'

Aae stopped to think. 'Just the same,' he said,

with a catch in his throat. He was silent for a moment and then shook his head.

'What?' Kham Ngai and Majan asked simultaneously.

'It's not the same.'

'Why did you say it was the same at first?'

'Then it was the same.'

The three of them began to laugh.

The next day Kham Ngai stood looking at the elephant.

It's true what Aae said, he thought. It's still missing something. He walked out of the shed and passed the tamarind tree before stopping to look at the river. He stared at the steep banks on the far shore and then went back into the shed. He climbed up onto the elephant and sat on the neck.

The elephant was hard and unyielding. Sitting on the neck, it did not feel like an elephant. It was just a dry piece of wood – heavy, passive and numb.

He came down to take another look. It's like this, he thought. The ears are about to flap. The trunk looks as if it is swinging. The legs are ready to step. And the shape is beautiful.

But it's still missing something. He was still thinking furiously when he went to bathe in the river and that night he could not get to sleep.

'You've got to look at a real elephant,' Boon Ham advised him the next day after Kham Ngai spoke of his feelings.

For some weeks Phlai Sut had been dragging logs in the forest behind the village. Every afternoon his mahout would ride him past the workshop on the way to cross the river to the Phaw Liang's house. The mahout would often invite Kham Ngai to ride along with him.

'No. You go ahead,' Kham Ngai would shake his head. After he had refused several times, the mahout stopped asking.

'Why don't you go?' Boon Ham asked. 'The elephant has to pass right in front of your house.'

Kham Ngai didn't utter a word, but in his heart he always felt sadness and regret whenever he saw Phlai Sut. People often told him that the mahout was a drunkard who worked the elephant without pity. Phlai Sut was cut by the hook and forced to work until he was tired and listless.

Some days, the villagers said, the mahout was so drunk he could not walk straight. He would try to climb on the elephant only to fall in a heap on the ground time after time. Phlai Sut would use his trunk to lift the mahout to his neck but the mahout couldn't stay on, his body so uncoordinated that he would soon slide off again.

'The greatest of mahouts,' people would say.

One day as Phlai Sut passed in front of the workshop, Kham Ngai yelled that he wanted to go along. As soon as Kham Ngai climbed on the elephant's back and sat on the saddle pad and the wooden block supporting the harness, the mahout said, 'You're very strange. When I invite you, you don't come. But when I don't ask you, then you want to come.'

Kham Ngai was fascinated by the elephant, as if he had never seen one before. He stared, absorbing all of the details from head to tail as if they were entirely new. The regular swaying of the mass underneath him provoked a feeling of gentle intimacy that made him feel exhilarated. The elephant waded across the river and climbed the far bank, stopping by the tamarind tree in front of Kham Ngai's house to let him off.

Kham Ngai rode home with the mahout several times. A young man in the carving workshop said that he had seen some black liquid oozing from Phlai Sut's temples between the eye and the ear.

'He's coming into musth.'

'How do you know?' Kham Ngai asked.

'I heard people talking.'

'It's nothing special. If he's going to come into musth, the mahout is sure to know.'

'You can't trust a drunken mahout.'

But Kham Ngai rode Phlai Sut home again. The elephant bent his hind legs backwards, shuffling on his knees as he cautiously descended the steep bank, his head rocking from side to side. As soon as Phlai Sut reached the gravel bed at the water's edge, he jerked to a stop and then backed up as a black cat hissed loudly, running away from a dog that was chasing it out of the bushes. The dog careered into the elephant's legs. Phlai Sut spun his body and lifted his trunk, rumbling his throat. The mahout kicked his feet and tugged the elephant's ear with his hook. The elephant shook his head and trumpeted. The mahout yelled and raked the elephant's forehead, digging deep scratches. Phlai Sut was very agitated and afraid. He started to run along the beach.

Kham Ngai leaned forward and pressed himself against the elephant's back, grasping the harness as tightly as he could with both hands. The elephant lifted his trunk high before charging forward, shaking his head furiously. His great ears slapped powerfully back and forth. The mahout sat up straight, slashing the sharp hook at Phlai Sut's forehead with all of his strength. He raised the hook high in the air with one hand and held tightly to the elephant with the other. When the elephant shook his head violently once again, the mahout used the hook to tear long slices in the muscles over the elephant's skull.

Bright red blood flowed as the metal head of the hook sank in and was tugged out. The mahout fell over the side of the elephant's neck. His left hand grasped the neck rope to keep from falling while his legs scrambled furiously for a foothold as he tried to climb back up. The point of the hook pierced Phlai Sut's ear and he jerked and lunged forward, roaring. The mahout lost his grip on the neck rope. The cutting edge of the hook in his right hand dragged the elephant's ear, slicing it open. The mahout was thrown off and landed in the sand. Kham Ngai was wild with fear – it had all happened so quickly that there was no way to have anticipated it.

Phlai Sut ran forward, black, oily liquid pouring from his temples. Kham Ngai was trembling. His arms rubbed so hard against the wooden block supporting the harness that they were scraped raw. The earth beneath him seemed to heave. He decided to jump off if the elephant charged into the water. But Phlai Sut turned and ran madly along the shore and then tried to climb the steep bank, but he always slid back down. His feet pawed against the crumbly ground, tearing off chunks of earth and trampling plants. He skirted the shore and then turned back to the earth wall and tried to scramble up the bank again, but he slid back down time after time.

Kham Ngai felt his heart pounding like a drum, at first slowly and then ever faster until it echoed, overwhelming everything around him.

He held on precariously, thinking to jump off many times, but he did not dare. He was reeling. He slithered forward onto the elephant's neck and grabbed the base of an ear with one hand and the neck rope in the other. He was shaking all over. His heart pounded with a heavy thud. His bare feet probed frantically for the neckrope. When he found it he slid the rope into the space between his big toe and the first toe and then stretched his legs to steady himself.

Kham Ngai calmed himself. As soon as his seat was firm, he felt something emanating from the elephant's neck. He was so excited that he lost his fear instantly. It was this feeling that was missing from the wooden elephant. That is what I wanted to know – the inherent warmth and gentleness of the elephant running uncontrolled under his body. It has being. It has flesh and blood. It has life and spirit. He sensed the peak of the elephant's vitality as it charged forth.

He felt the elephant's terror and trembling, its sadness and pain, at the moment when it spun and ran headlong into the river.

Kham Ngai forgot about jumping off. As the elephant charged through the water, cool drops splashed all over him. The elephant clambered up the opposite shore and ran through a vegetable patch, trying again to scramble up the slippery bank. Phlai Sut charged aimlessly as if he were blind, running back and forth across the river, feeling there was no way out.

Kham Ngai sensed that Phlai Sut was becoming weaker. His fear had been entirely replaced by a desire for knowledge. How far will the elephant go? he thought. I'll wait and see what he does.

He felt at peace even as the elephant was charging forward. There was a cool breeze in his face. The mass of muscle and blood underneath him heaved up and down. The spirit was worn down. The body so strong and the spirit so frail, the bravery and the patience – the feelings bound together. There was nothing separating him from Phlai Sut. He leaned close against the neck as if he were just a part of the elephant. It was not a combat. Nobody was doing anything to anybody, he thought. We've only come to meet each other, to know each other. We did not come to take from each other but to give to each other.

He felt the pace slacken until finally the tired animal shuffled to the shore. The elephant was breathing hard and walked very slowly onto the sand. Kham Ngai directed him towards the end of the beach where there was a wallow of sticky mud. The elephant's legs sunk up to his stomach until he could move his feet only with difficulty. He had moved only two or three steps before he was completely mired.

Kham Ngai let out a sigh and turned to look

behind him. He saw three or four of the Phaw Liang's workers carrying chains and metal hobbles coming towards him.

After that day Kham Ngai became even more moody than before. If anybody asked him about the elephant in musth, he would just sit silently. Sometimes he would get up and walk away.

'Is your work done already, Kham Ngai?' Boon Ham asked from behind a pile of unfinished statues. 'Do you feel like carving?'

Kham Ngai shook his head and looked outside distractedly. These days he was coming to the taxidermy room every day. As soon as his work was done, he would go outside and sit under the rain tree.

He had not entered the shed for a long time. After he climbed down from Phlai Sut's neck the day the elephant had run wild, Kham Ngai had felt just the opposite of what he had felt on the day when he had left the wooden elephant. On the last day with the statue he had felt relieved and happy, but after he had encountered the life force of Phlai Sut, he reverted to trembling and felt he had done nothing. He still remembered clearly the animal he had ridden – Phlai Sut possessed spirit, and everything that his wooden elephant lacked. Whenever he thought back to the days and nights he had spent in the shed with the block of rosewood, he felt only desolation and melancholy.

It was nothing but a hard, blunt piece of wood. It was the carcass of a dead tree. He brooded about the statue, his thoughts circling over and over again.

'What do you want?' Boon Ham asked. 'Do you want it to run? To trumpet? To drag logs?'

'It's not like that,' Kham Ngai said. 'Anyway, I didn't say that I wanted it to run.'

'What it is, well, that's enough. Don't think too much. Some people only want carcasses. They're not interested in life the way you like to talk about it.'

When Majan saw that he did not want to discuss the wooden elephant she asked, 'Aren't you going to work on it any more?'

He didn't answer but just sat quietly.

Aae came up from the river and asked, 'When are you going to make the tusks and the ladder?'

Kham Ngai sat silent and indifferent. He thought it peculiar that he had been totally obsessed by the wooden elephant for so long.

'I don't know why I made it,' he said to himself while staring at the sun disappearing behind the opposite shore. 'I was absorbed in it for many years.'

'Come on! Finish it up,' Majan said, 'and then go sell it to the Phaw Liang.'

The Phaw Liang had always liked huge wooden elephants. 'They give you a sense of power and strength,' he said to customers who came to admire the goods at the workshop. 'The bigger the log, the more fitting it is that it should be turned into an elephant.'

Why do men take blocks of wood and make them into elephants? Kham Ngai wondered. We human beings are strange. Wood always has a bigness of its own, and even when it is turned into an elephant, the bigness still comes from the tree – and not from the man who carves it. A big piece of wood, all it is really is just a tree. But people cannot see the beauty of a tree when it is standing and giving shade, so they chop it down, cut the branches and strip the leaves, turning it into a wooden corpse. And then they carve it into the corpse of an elephant, praising and admiring it more than a real elephant or a living tree. Turning this into that, that into this, until none of it is real, neither the tree nor the elephant.

The shed covering the elephant had screens of split bamboo on three sides while half of the fourth side was left open. Kham Ngai brought some teak boards and made a hinged door. The five panels folded together but they could also be extended to totally hide the elephant from sight.

'When I've got some free time I'll get back to work on it,' he told Majan and then allowed cobwebs to spread all over the inside, forming a curtain to the far corners.

Aae was now too old to enjoy playing with the elephant.
He showed no eagerness to even go and look at
it. The river held things far more interesting. He
would take his fishing pole and creel and wander
along the shore almost every day. Sometimes he
would wade neck high among floating plants and
catch shrimp with his dip net. Sometimes he would
dive to the muddy bottom for mussels and then
take them home for Majan to cook.

When Aae was so absorbed in his activities at
the river that he came home late, Majan would go
looking for him. She would follow the shoreline,
craning her neck impatiently and looking everywhere. The sound of her high-pitched shouts
echoed along the banks.

'What are you worried about?' the neighbours
would ask when they saw that she had not found
Aae. 'He swims like a fish.'

When the water was rising and there were loose
logs floating down from the north, Aae and his
friends would swim out to capture logs. They
would grab logs and paddle with their feet, pulling
the logs ashore. Sometimes the current would
sweep them far downstream. One day Aae had a
cramp and his body went into spasms. Luckily, his
friends pulled him ashore and laid him on the
ground. As soon as Aae's cramp had gone, they all
jumped back in the water, laughing loudly.

Aae's latest batch of ducklings had just hatched.

The same day, early in the morning, the river rose rapidly to halfway up its banks. Earthworms in great masses crawled up the bank to escape the water. Aae collected some, putting them in a coconut shell, and went home to feed the ducklings. Then he went to help Majan pick vegetables where the water was beginning to flood the garden. He took down the wicker fence and put it away. Then he grabbed his creel and his fishing pole and walked to the river.

He took a worm from the current, baited his hook and then climbed up on a raft that was moored to the shore. Just there, the water was placid because it was inside a long, broad curve. The current was swift only on the northern bank. Aae cast his line over the far side of the rafts. Several other rafts drifted downstream in front of him. Sometimes when rafts broke away from the current they would slowly drift into the quiet water and collide with the rafts already there. Aae spread his legs to steady himself to pull in a catfish on his line. Some rafts passed so close that Aae could hear the sound of the logs shifting. When other rafts struck Aae's, the logs would shudder and roll, making his footing unsteady.

When Aae had taken a fish off the hook and put it in his creel, he would immediately bait the hook again and cast it into the wake of a drifting log. Then a fish bit and Aae could not pull it up through the narrow space between logs. The fish wriggled until it slipped the hook. So Aae stepped over to a raft that had just come alongside. When he looked behind him, he saw logs scattered all along the bank for a long way. The new raft did not have anybody tending it so he concluded it had probably slipped loose and was floating by itself. It had been alongside for only a moment when the current shifted and the raft moved rapidly downstream. Aae jumped back to the first raft before the new one was swept into the middle of the river.

Aae cast his line over the side of the raft into water dazzling in the sun. His line was jerked down almost immediately in rapid twitches and then pulled under the water. Aae yanked the pole back. A catfish, its belly white, its back a shiny steel blue, leaped from the water with a splash.

When another raft of logs drifted close Aae shifted the tip of the pole towards it and hauled the fish in. The fish fell off the hook and flopped around on the logs so Aae had to scramble for it. The spined fin of the fish pierced deeply into the palm of his hand. He jolted, feeling a stabbing pain and then pulled at the fin with all his strength. The poisonous barb dug into muscle, and blood trickled from the hole, turning his palm bright red. The pain reached up his arm. He looked at the puncture with fear and tried to move, stepping on the slimy green moss on the side of a log. He slipped and fell, his head smashing against the hard wood. Curling up in pain, he tumbled over the side of the raft and sank underwater, descending at the same rate as a new raft that was drifting in. The raft covered the surface of the water above him.

People on the shore nearby yelled in panic. Kham Ngai had been waiting for a boat for hire to cross over to the workshop. He ran to the raft and saw the creel and fishing pole lying across the logs. In a moment he and the neighbours rushed to look for a pole to pry away the outside raft. People on the shore who had heard the shouting rushed to help. When the rafts were finally separated Kham Ngai dived under the water. He frantically groped everywhere and then emerged, his lungs empty. He went under again immediately, diving and surfacing many times. There seemed to be no hope but he would not stop. Men who had dived in to help grabbed him and forcibly pulled him back onto the raft. He shook himself free and dived under again. When he seemed no longer able to breathe, he grasped a partially submerged log and rested his head on the mossy surface.

One man fetched a casting net and repeatedly threw it around the side of the raft. The man worked feverishly until he was exhausted where-upon other men came and took turns, changing the casting place from the side of the raft to the stern. A large crowd had formed.

The shouting became louder when the net pulled in a body. People rushed to disentangle Aae from the net. They kneaded his swollen stomach, causing water to gush from his mouth. His face was dull grey and distorted, and there were beads of water all over his still body. A neighbour carried him to the shore and laid him on the sandy beach. They massaged his back and then his stomach. One old woman still believed in the local superstition that a drowned body could be revived by shaking it in a pan, so she ran home to get the battered one she used to winnow bran for her pigs. They put the boy face down into the large pan and spun it around. Then they shook it – but Aae still lay motionless. The frenzied mood gradually dissipated and the people became silent. They turned the limp body on its back and arranged it on the sandy beach devoid of hope.

Majan ran down the bank in alarm, her eyes wild with fear. Kham Ngai lifted Aae's body and placed it face down over his shoulder. He shook the body so that water poured out, walking back and forth. Then he started running in circles in the sunshine, which was gradually losing its soft lightness.

High above on the edge of the bank a group of people stood close together. When they looked down at the river's edge they saw a man carrying a boy over his shoulder, trotting in aimless circles.

Three or four steps behind there was a woman running after him.

Boon Ham raised his hammer to strike the chisel into the wood. As a shadow suddenly passed over him, he raised his face and shouted, 'Don't drop it!'

But he was too late. The man who had run bent over into the taxidermy room leaned his shoulder to let the carcass of a deer fall to the floor, then turned around and rushed out sobbing.

Boon Ham stuffed animals for many days, substituting for Kham Ngai, who had stopped coming to work. Kham Ngai's appearance was very gloomy. The face that had smiled so brightly was now always solemn.

'It's not right that he died,' Boon Ham said on the day of Aae's cremation, trying to console Kham Ngai. 'He practically lived in the water.'

'He probably got a cramp and swallowed water,' a villager said. 'I had one once. My body curled up and went hard.'

From the first moment, Aae's death caused Kham Ngai great grief. He was obstinate. He wouldn't let anybody near the boy's body. Nobody heard his moaning and sobbing. They only saw him hugging Aae tightly to his chest, rocking him in his arms as if he were singing a lullaby. He was stunned and perplexed and showed no interest in anything around him. When anybody came to talk to him about what to do with the body he would turn away and stare fixedly, not uttering a word, until the other person stopped talking. But friends and relatives made a great fuss of helping with everything, taking on various chores, and the cremation passed by smoothly.

'Get outside for a while,' Boon Ham said many days later, when he saw that Kham Ngai had not yet released his sorrow. 'It's not good to be stuck in the house – it'll just get worse.'

So Kham Ngai went to the workshop and worked very hard every day. Boon Ham stopped filling in for him, and gave him all of the taxidermy work as before. Kham Ngai toiled all day long. He did not talk to anybody, and he often stared blankly at the work in front of him and sighed.

One set of customers, acquaintances of the Phaw Liang, stopped off at the workshop quite frequently. They came from Bangkok and they always went into the forest as a group, hunting animals for many days.

'It's really too bad I missed that gaur,' one of the customers said outside the taxidermy room after just having come out of the forest. 'He ran very fast. I didn't have time to aim right.'

'You'll get one next time,' one of his friends said.

'His horns were really beautiful. I've got to go back for them.'

'You should talk to the taxidermist,' his friend said. 'He'll carve a form so as to be ready for the skin and horns.'

The hunter laughed and said, 'That's not a bad idea, you know.' He walked into the taxidermy room looking at the stuffed animals inside with such great interest that he did not see a dirty little boy coming through the door. He bumped into the child and sent him staggering.

Kham Ngai saw the same group again about a month later. As soon as their jeep was parked, five people jumped out, each carrying a rifle of strange design. They helped each other to lift a deer from the roof of the jeep and set it down in front of the shop. The deer was very beautiful, especially its antlers, which had many forks on both sides. The carcass was floppy and there was caked blood down its neck and chest. Another man carried in a langur, which was swaying in his grasp. There were several bullet holes in its torso.

The hunters chatted happily, full of pride.

As they were leaving, one man told Kham Ngai, 'Do a good job, okay? Make it beautiful.' After he had climbed into the jeep, he turned and yelled, 'Make it look as if it was really alive!'

Before the engine started, another hunter called

loudly, 'Have him stuff life into it! Then it'll really seem alive.'

The men laughed boisterously as the jeep drove away. A thick cloud of dust formed a curtain, and the driver almost didn't see a little boy who had to scurry out of the way. Kham Ngai stared at the back of the jeep until it vanished from sight.

'Stuff life . . .' Kham Ngai muttered, repeating the words he had just heard, and then sat smiling quietly to himself. Whenever he thought of those words, he could not help but be amused. He forgot his sorrow for a moment, chuckling softly. Boon Ham turned around, his face looking doubtful and confused.

'What's so funny, Kham Ngai?' he asked.

'Nothing,' Kham Ngai said, looking embarrassed. 'Where are those people from?'

When he saw that Boon Ham was still confused, he added, 'Those city people.'

'Oh, them. They're friends of the Phaw Liang.'

Kham Ngai stared at the dead deer and the langur and he sighed.

'What are you thinking of?' asked Boon Ham, still baffled.

'Nothing. Absolutely nothing.'

Kham Ngai was still thinking of the customer's phrase. 'That group was probably joking,' he told himself. 'Stuff life. How can you do that?' When he had thought about it for a while he wished it could be done. 'What would it be like if we could stuff life into lifeless things?'

He didn't want Boon Ham to know what he was thinking. If Boon Ham knew, he would surely laugh at him.

When he was still in school Kham Ngai had always remembered sayings and phrases that were catchy like that. He liked to say them himself. Sometimes his friends laughed at him and teased him, until he hung his head unhappily.

'Are those your words or somebody else's?'

'Did you remember that from a book?'

'Where did you pick that up? From your father or from a monk?'

His friends would all giggle.

But Kham Ngai liked to remember these over-heard phrases and use them when talking to his friends. He felt that such words and sayings carried meaning. They made him feel self-assured, even to the point of cockiness.

Later, when he was older, all the many experiences he had encountered made him understand that there was far more to life than catchy phrases. Things that he had never known, he had to know. Things that he had never seen, he had to see.

'Why are you so quiet?' Boon Ham asked when he saw Kham Ngai quietly staring at the carcasses the hunters had left on the stump in front of the shop.

Kham Ngai was thinking of Aae's body at the time when he had carried it over his shoulder. It had been so limp and so cold . . . so still. Kham Ngai trembled violently when he remembered those qualities, so different from the Aae that he had known. Aae's body had always felt warm and smiling. Breathing. But now, I know all those things are gone – the life is gone from him – he's just a carcass beginning to rot. There is no way to bring him back to life.

Kham Ngai stood up.

'Aren't you going to do any work today?' Boon Ham turned and looked at Kham Ngai, then helped him to move the pile of dead animals inside.

Kham Ngai stayed in the taxidermy room for a while and then, his face pale, came out again looking for Boon Ham.

'Can you give me a hand for a while?'

Boon Ham lifted his head and looked at him. 'Aren't you feeling well?'

Kham Ngai shook his head.

'You rest for a while,' Boon Ham said. 'I'll do it for you.'

Kham Ngai was trembling, though he didn't know why. I'm probably thinking about Aae too much, he told himself. When he cut open the langur's stomach to take out the guts, he couldn't stand it. When he glanced sideways at the langur, its eyelids were open as if it was staring at him.

How could I do this before? he thought. I have done so many animals and it never seemed anything special.

He thought of the way Aae had cleaned fish in the river. Nobody had ever taught him. He simply pulled the guts out and threw them back into the stream, and then he strung the fish on a line to carry them home. It was a very natural thing to do, something normal and everyday. Those fish were food, he thought, so there was nothing strange about it. But sometimes animals were not food. He thought of the carcasses he had stuffed. Nobody ate that meat. It did not help to keep people alive.

'Do you like stuffed animals, Boon Ham?' he asked abruptly.

Boon Ham gave him a bewildered look. 'Why are you asking?'

'No special reason. I don't understand myself.'

'You don't understand what?'

Kham Ngai sat silently. He wanted Boon Ham to understand but didn't know what to say. He felt indifferent when he saw people butchering wild animals for food. As soon as it was done, everybody would sit around together and eat. Nobody talked about beauty. Nobody tried to make the carcass look as if it was still alive.

All of the stuffed animals had once been alive, he thought. They were flesh and blood. They had a spirit. And then they were shot. And then somebody came and made them look as if they were still alive.

People are strange, he thought. We kill animals and scoop out their guts. We pluck out their hearts and throw them away. And then we stuff them. And only then do we look for life.

'How can you destroy life in order to create life?' he asked.

'You think too much,' Boon Ham said.

Kham Ngai was quiet. He thought of the customer who had complained that it was a shame he hadn't shot the gaur – and had then said it was beautiful. That is strange, to see that something is beautiful and then want to kill it. I must have misheard him. That bunch must have been happy that the gaur was still alive. But then why say it was a shame that he hadn't shot him? I don't understand at all.

One day when Kham Ngai was driving a load of stuffed animals and carvings to town, he met a funeral cortege that was moving in a long line down the middle of the road. The mourners were carrying candles and incense in their hands, walking very slowly. There was no room to pass on the sides so Kham Ngai slowed down and followed them. After a while, he looked behind and saw more people carrying candles and incense. He was in the middle of a procession moving very slowly to the temple. The next day he told Boon Ham.

'It was just as if those people were mourning the stuffed animals in our truck.'

'You are really very strange,' Boon Ham said. 'When will you learn to control yourself a little? Aae's been dead a long time now.'

But Kham Ngai always felt that Aae had left at just that moment. He dreamt of him often and with great happiness, but as soon as he awoke he was faced with an empty house, and his happiness disappeared with the dream.

One night he saw Aae riding a wooden elephant. When he woke, Kham Ngai was very excited and tried to recall the images so that he could describe the dream to Majan. He wasn't certain if Aae was riding the elephant to come looking for him, but he was certain that it was the elephant he had carved. He could tell because the feet were still only rough hewn wood.

When he had finished recounting the dream, Majan was indifferent, showing no emotion. In the past, she had always been attentive when she knew he had dreamed and she had always asked him to describe it.

When they were newly married, he had told her about when he was a boy and like to chase wisps of fog on the knoll behind the house. It was great fun and the whole world had seemed very beautiful.

'And now – are you still chasing fog?' she asked, smiling. 'You must have gathered a lot by now.'

He laughed shyly. 'Yes.' After a moment he said, 'I dream, too.'

'Good dreams or nightmares?'

He smiled and said that he dreamed of her grasping for wisps of fog, running gracefully after them.

'What did I put them in?' she asked directly, wanting to know.

'I forgot to look,' he answered. 'I only saw you gather them. If they were gold, you'd be very rich now.'

She tilted her face up and laughed. 'All of my secrets are gone.'

When she stopped laughing, she said, 'I'd like to be in that dream. But would there be anybody to come and help me? Would anybody want to?'

He hadn't dreamed like that for a long time, since Aae had died.

'Majan,' he uttered softly. He was silent again when he saw that she had turned back to her weaving. She had barely lifted her head to glance at him. She sat there throwing the shuttle across the warp as her feet moved the treadle, separating the long threads while at the same time pulling in on the weft. The sound was loud and rhythmical.

When there was no work to do she would gaze around aimlessly. In the house she was quiet. They hardly spoke except when friends came to visit, and even then the two of them listened far more than they spoke.

Majan went to visit her mother in the northern part of the province, staying for many days. The afternoon she came home Kham Ngai saw her coming up the stairs carrying a small bamboo basket over her arm, as she always did when she went visiting. She seemed to be coping better though she was still quiet and solemn.

She tried to work all the time so there would be no empty moments. Every morning and afternoon she was busy along the shoulder of the bank, watering and spading the garden and picking vegetables. She had gotten more pigs to raise, and she still managed to weave almost every day.

On the day she had stopped working at the store in town to come and live with Kham Ngai, all of her friends tried to warn her against it.

'Keep working! It's a lot of fun here,' they said.

'I'm married already,' she said.

'Even if you're married you can still work.'

But she gave up work. There were times when she was lonely in the house on the shores of the Yom River. She missed her friends from town. The store was always fun and comfortable and wonderfully cool from the air-conditioning. There were always people coming and going, and there was always the sound of laughter. And the store was safe, in spite of the frightening stuffed animals.

'In a while you'll come to know,' her friends said, 'that life outside is difficult.'

What her friends had said was true, she thought, after a long time. Life outside the store was not like working in the store. Even though there were the same kinds of animals, outside they were alive and they had teeth that could bite and claws that could scratch. Majan knew that she had become more reflective now than when she had worked in the store. And she had only to look at her thickened, work-worn hands to know that it had not been an easy life.

Whenever they met afterwards, upon seeing her shabby living conditions, her friends would teasingly ask, 'How is it going? It's hard, isn't it?'

She would simply smile.

'We told you, but you didn't believe us,' her friends said. 'Do you regret coming here?'

She would shake her head in denial when she thought of the Yom River and the tall banks which were so familiar to her.

'No. Things are the way they are.'

Majan felt a little strange about herself for having been able to live by the river for so long. She came to realise that sometimes people do more than they ever thought they could do, and they sometimes become more than they could ever have foreseen.

'Let's go to the knoll,' Kham Ngai said gently when he saw her sighing and hiding her feelings.

Majan stood up from the loom and then walked out from under the house. Hugging her shoulders, she walked alongside Kham Ngai as they passed by the tamarind tree and took the path towards the knoll. A cold wind had been blowing for many days already, and when they came out into the open they saw drifts of fog covering the top of the knoll.

They climbed to the top, their feet leaving light trails in the dew-covered grass. When they entered the soft whiteness, they felt moisture against their faces. They sat on a rock beneath a tree on the crest of the knoll staring at the fine mist diffused all around. Drops of fog nuzzled their faces and clung to their hair.

The tree overhanging the rock was a vibrant green and its branches spread wide overhead. It was a very big and tall tree and the leaves were sprouting. Some of the time they could see the foliage and some of the time they could not see it at all. Mostly they could see only flashes of leaves between whirls of fog, and at first they could not even tell if the tree was flowering.

It flowered only once a year, in the hot season, and it flowered suddenly, the blossoms disappearing just as quickly as they had come. It mystified Kham Ngai that one day the tree would be covered in green leaves and the next day the leaves would be gone, all fallen to the ground. Then, immediately, yellow petals would burst forth, thickly covering the branches and trunk. The yellow was bright and lustrous.

The flowers fell just as quickly as the leaves. The petals dropped to the base of the trunk until the ground was brilliant yellow. The next day there would not be a trace of yellow on the tree but only naked twigs and branches in the sweltering air.

'It flowers so quickly,' he said, describing the succession to Majan. 'The blossoms pop out and then drop. I wish they would stay so I could look at them for a long time.'

'It's an ugly tree,' she said. 'What's it called?'

'I don't know the name,' he said. 'Forget it.'

Majan's feelings about the tree reminded Kham Ngai of the time before they were married when she sometimes told him of her fears about the future. Life had always been a frightening thing to her. She doubted there was any beauty in it.

'Look over there.' Kham Ngai pointed to a rainbow, as excited as a child. The fog bank had lifted, leaving a vivid arc of colours hanging in the air so close he thought he could reach out and touch it.

That night she dreamed that she was sitting on the knoll with Kham Ngai.

'Fog has substance, doesn't it? Then why can't we touch it?' In the dream her voice was soft and gentle. 'Because if it doesn't have substance, then how can we see it?'

Kham Ngai became very animated. 'We should collect some of it.'

'Collect it and put it in what?'

'Anything.'

'A basket?'

'A basket would be good.'

She did not ask what reason there could be for collecting fog. There was no time to ask – she had to hurry before the fog dissolved completely.

'Let's go and catch it right now before it's too late!' she said, though as she spoke she realised that they had only their bare hands. She started to cry softly and turned to walk into the disappearing fog as the sunlight grew rapidly brighter. Majan woke from the dream and furtively used the back of her hand to wipe her tears.

That afternoon when Kham Ngai got home from the workshop he saw her swinging a bush knife at a stand of bamboos.

'What are you doing?'

'I want to make a basket.'

He stood quietly for a moment and then put out his hand to take the knife from her. He cut some stalks of bamboo and then split them into an armful of thin strips, which he then smoothed. After that he often saw her sitting in front of the shed plaiting the long strips. She wove with great serenity. Many times she finished a basket only to tear it apart and weave it again. Sometimes she would fetch an old basket to study the design. She buried her grief in her work as she tried to stop thinking of Aae. Concentrating on the task in front of her, it took her many days to make a finished basket. It was beautiful and had an intricate pattern around the edge and on the lid.

She shyly held it up to show Kham Ngai and laughed.

'What's it for?' he asked.

'For gathering fog.'

He felt happy and told her, 'Make one for me, too!'

'We'll use this one together,' she said. 'What do we need two for?' She smiled demurely and stepped into the shed, hanging the basket from the elephant's trunk. Then she turned and went back to the house without saying a word.

When Kham Ngai got to work the next morning he greeted Boon Ham very cheerfully, but by that afternoon he was moody again.

'Why do we have to come here every day to carve statues and stuff these animals?' Kham Ngai asked.

Boon Ham set down his chisel, looked up, and began to laugh.

'You should have asked that question years ago,' he said. 'I'll tell you why. We make them so we can sell them – people come to buy and we sell.'

That's right, Kham Ngai thought, as he walked to the cupboard where the skins were stored. I make them because people come and buy them. Nobody cares whether they are alive or not. The buyers want carcasses around to look at every once in a while. All I do is slow down the process of decomposition. It's good, really, that there is no way to stuff life. If it were possible to bring carcasses back to life, things would get very complicated for me. People would probably want all kinds of things to be stopped and not allowed to continue on their path.

I don't understand the customers. Those big city people think in a way that I can't quite understand. If they came and saw the fog and a rainbow, as I have seen, what would they feel? They would surely be excited – but it's better if they don't see it anyway. After a while they would want to stuff that as well.

If the customers want me to stuff some fog or to stuff a rainbow, what should I do? I have no idea, really. I would end up chasing rainbows until the day I die.

And after that I'd have to stuff months. Stuff years. Immobilise them for a while so they don't move on. It's really good luck that there has never been a customer to order anything like that. All I've ever had to stuff is dead animals.

Let it go, he thought. Don't think about it too much. But even the simple stuffed animals; I can't do it any more. I'm trembling all over. I'm sorry for all of that life that was plucked away. I can't help those animals. I've reached the point where I'm always sad and discouraged. What is this feeling? Why have I just come to realise it? Aae knew all this long before me. He knew it the day his duckling died. I didn't have a clue then. I was too busy carving the elephant – I wanted to make something big.

He tried to think of a reason why he should keep on stuffing animals. He was afraid to lose his job, but in the end he decided.

'I can't do it anymore,' he told Majan when he got home from work.

She listened to him quietly and then slowly nodded her head. 'Stop working for a while,' she said with a sigh. 'But you've got to do something else if we're going to manage.'

He didn't answer. The afternoon he had decided to quit, he had not considered what other sort of work he would do. It was only after he got home that he began to think of how he could keep busy. For many mornings after he quit, he unexpectedly felt a certain emptiness at the time he used to briskly set off for a hard day's toil at the workshop. Now, from the moment he opened his eyes in the morning, he was faced with many long hours to fill.

'There's a lot of work to do around the house,' Majan said when she saw that all he did was to sit moping.

He helped her to water the vegetable garden and to tend the pigs and ducks every morning and every afternoon. But that was quickly done and the middle of the day stretched on forever. He was by himself so much that he could hardly endure it. Whenever he saw Majan weaving industriously, he thought of going and finishing the rosewood elephant, but he felt too tired to pick up his hammer and chisel again.

Before, when he had been carving the elephant, he had always felt there was too little time to get the work done. But now there was too much time. Time had no significance, and every place seemed filled with emptiness. A void awaited him in the sunlight and in the dark. The days followed each other so much alike that he began to cower.

'I want to stuff them, these damned days and nights,' he told Majan. 'Then they wouldn't be so bloody empty.' He turned to go downstairs, leaving Majan to stare at his back in bewilderment. But who, he thought, could stop the emptiness? Oh, it'll pass. It's just life – you can't bring it to a standstill. He thought of Aae. He thought of Aae's vitality and high spirits. That was all gone. He thought of Aae's corpse, a carcass with no meaning. Anything that can be preserved indefinitely is just a carcass.

Why is it impossible to preserve life? It probably is possible, he thought, but you would certainly have to know the right method. I would really like to know – if you're going to preserve life, how do you do it?

'Well, to start with, you don't kill it,' he said out loud, only to be startled by his own voice. He looked all around him to see if anybody was near enough to have overheard, but when he saw that he was alone he continued to think as he walked along the river bank.

Part of it is easy, he thought. If you want to preserve life, then you have to watch over it. Love it. Cherish it. And doing all of that is a lot easier than stuffing life back into a carcass.

He went down to the river. The level had started to drop and the water was getting turbid. He saw the beauty of the light scintillating off the muddy water. He felt he would like to run again one more time when he turned and saw the dog with the sore back. His heart rose when he saw the dog, but he felt too tired to run, and so he sat down and patted the dog until it grew bored. The dog jumped up and wagged its tail at him, though only for a moment, and then ran off. The sense of well-being that had arisen soon disappeared, and Kham Ngai became as depressed as before.

People who passed in front of his house in the morning were likely to see him sitting vacantly at the top of the steps, his elbows on his knees, his chin resting on his hands. He would sit under a betel nut vine of a deep and glossy green, the leafy tendrils thickly covering the trellis to which they were clinging. The beads of dew on the leaves were round and glittering. Kham Ngai would sit there quietly under the arbour until he could hear Majan's voice call from downstairs, 'Come and help me carry the food for the pigs!' or 'Help me water the garden!' Then he would get up.

In the rainy season Kham Ngai felt the emptiness ebb slightly because he could work in the rice fields every day. But once the planting was done he would be idle again until harvest time. He tried to keep busy doing a bit of this and a bit of that. Sometimes he went fishing down at the river. And when the season changed and there were more fish, he would often go to the rapids with friends.

Scattered along both banks of the river were people who had come to catch fish. Most of them had casting nets but some had dip nets and some had scoop nets. Many people had come from villages far from the river, and a few had even built temporary huts, settling down for a whole month to make salted fish.

Every year at this time the fish migrated up-stream. Upon reaching the rapids they would try to fight through the cascade, jumping and then falling back heavily into the spume or onto the boulders. There were fish of all sizes, from the little mud carp and snakehead mullet to big rock catfish and white sheat fish, all trying to force their way upstream through the frothy white water. When they were fresh they leaped from the water, their bellies flashing in the sun. When they were at the end of their strength they would float down to rest in the quiet pools behind the boulders. Some of the fish jumped many times, hovering in the air, before they were able to get over the boulders into the deep, still water above the rapids.

One day as Kham Ngai was hopping across the boulders in the river, carrying a casting net in his hands, he tripped and fell into the frothy water. 'Grab the rope!' his friends shouted, almost as soon as he had slipped off the boulder. He had fallen into the pull of a swift current which gushed in frothing bubbles and pulled the net from his hands. He bobbed around, crashing into a funnel trap for catching fish and ricocheting into the circular mouth of the net, which was entirely submerged. The torrent flooded over his face as he clung to the rim of the net, his legs flailing around behind him. The mouth of the net was supported by a frame made of large pieces of bamboo, and the body of the net stretched behind in a vast sack. The swift current swept everything into the sack. Even the strongest fish could not fight the current to escape – when the net was lifted out it would be full of dead fish.

Kham Ngai clung to the mouth of the net trying to pull himself out, struggling against the pummelling flow. He tried to wriggle out. The roaring water surging around the boulders drowned out all other sounds. He was very cold and he felt he had been underwater for a long time, so long that he wouldn't be able to come back. He tried desperately to hold his breath. His hands were cramped from clinging to the rim of the net, and his arms turned rigid from fatigue. He didn't hear anything and he didn't see anything. Then there arose an urge to fight. All his being concentrated on struggling to escape from the current battering against him. His heart was beating like a drum, the rhythm at first slow but gradually building to a staccato beat. He turned his face directly into the current, forcing his nose and mouth up, looking for air. Then, with a final push he thrust his body above the water and grabbed a support post and pulled himself from the net.

He curled himself around the bamboo pole, head down and mouth open, gasping for air. He didn't see the people running to crowd around and watch him from the boulders. Some of the men were working their way towards the net with knives so that they could cut the ropes holding it to the frame.

Kham Ngai released his grip and kicked himself away from the fish trap. He floated to the foot of the rapids then slowly paddled to the shore and sat on a rock. He was exhausted and his sodden clothes clung to him. His heart pounded. He lifted his hands to wipe the water from his face and then stood up and took his clothes off to wring them out.

A friend hopped over the rocky beach and came up to him.

'How are you?'

'Oh,' Kham Ngai said nodding his head and smiling, 'it was nothing.'

That's right, he thought. It was nothing. It was my duty to get out of that net. Nobody came in time to help, so I had to get myself out. He thought of the fish leaping over the rapids. It was very strange. How were they able to thrust their bodies against the current like that? They were so strong and agile. The ones who simply floated along with the current were likely to be dead fish before long.

'They must be going somewhere,' Kham Ngai told his friend over the roar of the rapids. 'Before getting there how many rapids do they have to pass? How many fish traps? How many nets?'

His friend laughed and said, 'You're talking as if you were a fish.'

'It's good luck that I'm not a fish.' He was quiet for a moment and then turned to look his friend in the eye. 'But, then again, I'm not sure – maybe my luck is worse than theirs.'

'Worse luck than a fish?'

'I might meet bigger rapids and bigger nets than this.'

'Then don't come and live in this river.' Kham Ngai's friend was amused. His face reflected the humour of the situation as he said, 'Move to another river!'

'Which river?'

'A river with no rapids and no nets.'

'Is there a river like that?'

The friend laughed raucously, though the sound could barely be heard above the roaring of the river.

'I'm going home,' Kham Ngai said.

'Come on! Stay and fish a bit more.'

'I've got enough already. What do I need more for?' Kham Ngai looked at the fish he had caught.

A year earlier Kham Ngai and this friend had made a funnel trap together at a time when the water was rising. The two of them had taken a small boat and driven big poles into the middle of the river in front of Kham Ngai's house. They tied the bow of the boat to a pole and then lowered the bottom of the net to the river bed, leaning the lifting handle of the net against the bow of the boat. There were a lot of fish, and they hoisted the full net repeatedly until they were tired. The little boat was very heavily loaded but Kham Ngai's friend said, 'One more haul and that's enough.' Then, 'Come on, just a little bit more.' He had forgotten everything else in his delight at having caught so many fish. When his friend finally untied the boat from the pole, Kham Ngai was tending the stern and he started throwing fish overboard so as to reduce the load. His friend shouted angrily, and Kham Ngai answered, 'Can't you see the boat is overloaded?'

'What a shame. All those beautiful fish.'

'We can't take them all – it's just a little boat.'

'Yes, but I want them,'

The instant the bow of the boat drifted away from the pole it was hit broadside by the torrent. It began to rock and keel over until water poured in. The boat rocked harder and started to sink. As the water entered the boat, Kham Ngai struggled to keep the boat upright – he was determined to keep it afloat. Water spilled in reaching the gunwales and the boat flipped over, bottom side up.

He sank underwater, his legs thrashing about aimlessly. He drifted and then was suddenly pulled straight down. There was nothing he could do but accept the vastness and depth of the river and his own smallness and fragility.

After drifting downstream to quiet water, Kham Ngai and his friend swam after the paddles which had slipped from their hands. When they found the boat, they turned it over and then rocked it to slosh the water out over the sides, at the same time treading with their feet to push the boat ashore.

There was not a single fish left in the boat.

Whenever he told this story, Kham Ngai would shake his head. 'I don't know why we had so many fish. We only eat a few.'

'People will come and buy a lot,' somebody would always say, 'if you can bring them in.'

'Sure,' Kham Ngai invariably answered, 'if you can bring them in.'

Majan sat in the blacksmith's shack with her legs dangling behind the forge, her arms moving the handle of the bellows up and down. Puffs of air entered the simple furnace and the burning charcoal flared brightly. Kham Ngai used tongs to pick a red-hot iron bar out of the furnace and hold it on the anvil. He lifted his hammer and struck, beating out the shape of a knife blade. He turned the blade over to examine both sides before nestling it back in the coals one more time.

'It's unbelievable that Phlai Sut's tusks are gone,'

Majan said as she pulled the bellows handle. 'How did they ever manage to steal them?'

'Cut them off with a saw.'

'That can't be easy to do.'

'People do it all the time. When they've got no money, some people will even cut off the tusks of their own elephant and sell them.'

'There's a ceremony you have to do before you cut. I've seen it. The person cutting the tusks must bless the tools. Sometimes the elephant isn't willing and it has to be put into a crush and held tightly before you can cut.'

'Yes, but these days there's powerful anaesthetics you can inject them with,' Kham Ngai said, squatting by the furnace. 'And there are electric saws – you don't even have to move your hands.'

'I feel sorry for him.'

Kham Ngai would stop off to see Phlai Sut almost every day, treating his wounds and shooing flies away. He would mutter soft words of consolation to the elephant, which was kept in a shed beside the Phaw Liang's house.

Phlai Sut was drowsy and listless, and his condition deteriorated rapidly. He seemed unaware of what was happening around him. His tail never swished and his trunk hung limp. His eyes were glazed. Kham Ngai would sigh loudly as he washed out the wounds. Phlai Sut's tusks were symbolic of his majesty, his status, his pride and his sense of self – but all of that had been stolen from him.

'Well, there's nothing left,' he said to himself, 'except for a worn-out body. He's pathetic.'

Some days Kham Ngai massaged the base of the massive legs, feeling that he wanted to tell him something. I'm like you, Phlai Sut, he thought. I don't have tusks any more either.

Phlai Sut's mahout had furtively left the village, not daring to face the Phaw Liang. Some people even said that the mahout had connived with the thieves who had cut the tusks.

'That bastard probably wanted revenge for the day he was thrown from the elephant,' Boon Ham said.

'When?' a villager asked. 'Way back then? That was a long time ago.'

'Yes, but he's the type to bear a grudge.'

'It was evil people who did that to Phlai Sut.'

Gradually Phlai Sut got better. Kham Ngai would take him to the river to bathe, scrubbing him all over, and he always brought some sugar cane or bananas. It was several months before Phlai Sut was back to normal. Then the Phaw Liang sent somebody to ask Kham Ngai to be Phlai Sut's mahout. Kham Ngai was in great turmoil.

'Should I do it?' he asked Majan.

'It's better to do blacksmithing here at home,' Majan said. 'Or don't you like it?'

'I like it.'

'Then why go off wandering? If you're here in the rainy season we can help each other in the rice fields.'

The picture that stayed in Kham Ngai's mind was of him and Phlai Sut playing together when they were children. Phlai Sut was a friend. Kham Ngai could see the big ears opening wide, the trunk waving gracefully, and the handsome legs ambling with that long, swaying stride.

'I really miss him,' he told Majan.

After sitting and thinking for nearly a week, he was still agitated. Then one evening he lay in bed with his eyes open, unable to sleep. At dawn he grabbed his hook and his bush knife, went downstairs, and set off to work for the Phaw Liang. Kham Ngai and Phlai Sut left the village to work together in a forest where many trees were being cut down. After they had dragged logs in the forest for a month, the Phaw Liang ordered Kham Ngai and Phlai Sut to come home and shift the logs in the meadow to the river bank.

'Drag that log over here for me first,' Boon Ham said, after they had eaten lunch together under the rain tree in front of the workshop. He pointed to the huge teak log by the bank. Kham Ngai climbed up on the elephant's neck and then turned.

'Wait a while,' Kham Ngai said, 'First, I've got to move those logs over to the river.'

'I've got to start carving that teak log. Come on, help me get the job moving faster.'

'You're always in a hurry. I can't go any faster than I am already.'

'You can!'

'If it's like that, go drag it yourself.'

Kham Ngai nudged the elephant into a walk. Whenever he sat on Phlai Sut's neck, Kham Ngai felt totally at home, as if it was a special place only for him. When dragging logs the two of them were each like a part of the other. When Phlai Sut was tired, Kham Ngai was tired. When Phlai Sut was troubled, Kham Ngai was troubled. When the elephant was working to the limits of his strength, Kham Ngai was doing the same.

Phlai Sut had been pulling steadily. Then he suddenly jerked, breaking his smooth rhythm. His feet scrambled rapidly as if he were about to run. Kham Ngai was jolted and the log was instantly jerked into motion. Kham Ngai turned to look behind and saw Boon Ham brandishing a wooden spear with a metal point, laughing loudly.

'Are you crazy?' Kham Ngai berated him loudly after returning to the workshop.

Boon Ham laughed again. 'You said you couldn't work any faster. I was just showing you that you could.'

'Don't you have any work to do? Nothing better to do than to pull stunts like that?'

'He moved much faster. Didn't you notice?' Boon Ham said. 'Do you want some more help? I'm free right now.'

'It would be better if you stayed in the workshop.'

'You should drag that hunk of teak over here for me.'

'Why are you in such a rush?'

'The Phaw Liang is pushing me. Pretty soon there's going to be five craftsmen showing up.'

'What kind of craftsmen?'

'Woodcarvers to carve a big elephant. The Phaw Liang has hired them to help.'

'Having so many people, won't that just make it harder to do?'

'Not at all. They've got modern tools. There's a gouger that cuts wood as if it was dirt – just a second and it's all done.'

They can really do that, Kham Ngai thought, wading through the river to go home. Everything is changing so fast. When I was carving my elephant I had to struggle by myself. There was nobody to help me. But now they work in a bunch. If I told them how difficult it was for all of those years, they would laugh at me.

Kham Ngai directed the elephant off the path and had him stand still when he saw a child dragging a shovel at the head of a line of waddling ducklings, their stomachs stuffed. He instantly thought of Aae. The ducklings scattered, scurrying past the elephant's feet to hide in the grass at the side of the path. Even though he made the elephant stop, the ducklings would still not quiet down. But finally the child managed to round up the ducklings and soon, still quacking with fright, they disappeared.

'I'm going to drag that log,' Kham Ngai told Majan as he pointed to the big block of teak on the rim of the opposite bank. The sun was beginning to disappear behind the hilltops, dousing them with pastel colours.

'It's huge,' Majan said. 'Can you drag it?'

'Tomorrow we'll see.'

The next morning he stepped directly from Phlai Sut's neck across to the block of teak. He inspected the log for a moment and then jumped down to attach the drag chains to the nose holes. When Kham Ngai urged the elephant forward, he pulled stubbornly until the chains were taut but still the log would not budge. Phlai Sut backed up and started again, straining until his shoulders lowered.

Kham Ngai got down and released the chains

from the log. 'Let it sit for a while,' he said, and they went to drag logs from the meadow to the bank.

In the afternoon they tried again. Kham Ngai carefully studied the ground at the front of the log and then grabbed a pole and tried to lever it up until his muscles ached. He pushed as hard as he could but the log did not move, so he went back to the shade of the rain tree to fetch Boon Ham to have a look.

'It's not heavy,' Boon Ham said. 'It's big around but short.'

Phlai Sut tried again but the log would not move. Kham Ngai looked at the log thoughtfully, and then turned to speak to Boon Ham.

'We've got to use rollers. The elephant will be able to pull the log as if it had wheels.'

The two of them placed round branches in front of the log, but still it would not move. Kham Ngai let out a deep sigh and jumped off the elephant.

'We've got to get some help preparing the ground,' Boon Ham said.

'It should have been left at the workshop in the first place,' Kham Ngai said as he stood exhausted, contemplating the teak log. 'I don't know why they left it here.'

'When the logs were floated down from the north the Phaw Liang never thought he'd use it to make an elephant. He was going to cut it up into big boards right here.'

'If it's like that, then why don't you carve the elephant right here?'

'Out in the open like this? The heat would kill us.'

'Make an awning over it.'

'If it floods how would we get it out of here?'

'It won't flood. It doesn't flood every year.'

'Listen, I'm telling you it's better to carve it at the shop.'

Kham Ngai climbed up to untie the drag chains from the log. He was exhausted. The bark on top was very slippery and his feet skidded out from under him. He caught his fall with his hands, but his stomach thudded into the hard wood and he fell to the ground, curled up.

He pressed his hand to his stomach to stop the pain. Boon Ham rushed over to help him to his feet, but Kham Ngai waved him away. He took a deep breath and the sharp pain in his stomach ebbed. As his blurred vision cleared Kham Ngai looked to the side and saw the dirty little boy sucking his thumb and staring at him.

Boon Ham turned to walk to the workshop, and Kham Ngai climbed back up on the elephant. As he rode away he saw that the boy was following him with his eyes. In a flash he thought of Aae. And then he thought back to the boy. He had never taken any interest in him even though he had seen him often. Why don't I know him? It's strange. He must live nearby. Boon Ham must know who he is.

He recalled a time when he was still stuffing animals and the boy had come in and circled around him staring. Kham Ngai had gruffly shouted at him, 'Don't mess with those animals or I'll stuff you – to the very top!'

The boy had run headlong out the door.

Boon Ham had laughed and turned to say, 'You don't have to stuff him. He was so scared he looked as if he'd been stuffed already!'

At the time Kham Ngai had laughed very hard. It was strange that he had taken no interest in the boy. He had only seen him moving vaguely in the background.

As soon as he got back to the workshop he asked Boon Ham, 'Do you know the brat?'

Boon Ham was bewildered for a moment, but then he shook his head. 'I see him around here, but I don't know who he belongs to.'

Kham Ngai returned to the teak log again, but the boy was not there. Nobody else at the workshop knew the boy, though everybody had seen him running and playing nearby.

'He's got to have a mother and a father,' Kham Ngai said. 'Who else could he be living with?'

The next day a villager watering vegetables on the bank told him, 'I've seen him hanging around the temple. He probably lives there.'

'It's really quite sad,' a monk told Kham Ngai when he went to enquire at the temple. 'I have no idea where his parents have gone. They'll probably never come back.'

The following day Kham Ngai met the boy on his way home from work. He dismounted and kneeled, looking into the begrimed face for a long time.

'Do you want to come and live with me?' he asked, as the boy stood quietly sucking his thumb. Kham Ngai smiled at him and felt a sense of familiarity.

'Let's go,' Kham Ngai said, nodding his head towards the elephant. He picked the boy up and put him on the elephant's neck. He held the skinny child firmly on his lap as they went down the steep bank and crossed the river to go home.

Why wasn't I aware of this before, he thought, remembering the day Boon Ham had said the boy looked like a stuffed animal.

'But you're alive, aren't you?' Kham Ngai said to the boy.

I have been so busy taking care of things that don't have life that I have forgotten about taking care of things which are still alive. The body in his lap was warm. Kham Ngai's heart felt at peace. He had so wanted to carry Aae on his lap on this elephant a long time ago.

'What's your name?' he asked softly, bending down to look at the face. The boy's lips were closed tight, but he looked back quite openly. Kham Ngai looked intently for a moment and then nodded his head.

'Of course. How would you know? It's up to me to give you a name.'

He wrapped his arms tightly around the child, holding him to his chest.

That evening Majan bustled about, first taking the boy to the river for a good scrubbing and then making him dinner and a place to sleep. She watched over the boy until he slept.

'He's had a hard time,' Kham Ngai said to himself the next morning as he was attaching the chains to the log. He's just a very little boy. Nobody knows who he is. He has been deserted and left on his own. He has had to struggle with hunger and fear and it must have been very hard for him, like me when I'm pulling logs. I've had fear and hunger oppressing me. I've had to drag logs everyday. I didn't dare abandon those logs.

Thinking furiously he flicked the hook in his hands and nudged the elephant into motion with his knees. And what about Phlai Sut? Why does he have to haul logs? He should be off eating grass and fruit in the forest instead of drudging like this. What is he afraid of? What is forcing him? His eyes glanced down at the large domes of Phlai Sut's forehead and he saw many old scars. He's been driven the same way, he thought. Kham Ngai looked at the hook in his hands. Was he afraid of the hook? It would be funny if that were true – because Phlai Sut had been afraid for so long that he had become used to obeying orders. The hook was no longer needed. He worked willingly.

I'm just like Phlai Sut, he thought. I'm so afraid of the hook that I'm broken in to it. I don't dare do anything different. But the hook that scares me is invisible, just like the banks of a river in flood.

He looked behind and saw the log scraping up dirt. Do other people drag logs like I do?

What would it be like if that log behind me became invisible? Phlai Sut and I would still be pulling so hard that our bodies would contort with strain in the sunlight – yet anybody watching us would laugh their heads off. Boon Ham would think it was funny too. Today I'd like to invite him to come along.

'Come on, Boon Ham, let's go work the elephant together,' he teased Boon Ham when he stopped for a rest in the shade of the rain tree.

'Not for me. I'm a carver,' Boon Ham said. 'I don't drag logs like you.'

'You do drag logs. Absolutely everybody drags logs,' Kham Ngai said loudly. 'But they're invisible logs.'

He wanted to say that every human being had

a hook poised over their head, everybody had chains trailing behind them. But when he saw the confusion on Boon Ham's face, he decided not to say anything more.

The huge block of teak had been dragged almost six feet and then it stuck firm as before.

'At least it's shifted already,' Boon Ham said. He had been standing by the side of the log as Kham Ngai prodded Phlai Sut with his feet, his shoulders hunched down on the elephant's neck. Boon Ham said, 'I'll go and cut some more poles to use as rollers. You might as well go and drag from the meadow in the meantime.'

They returned to the meadow and dragged logs. The elephant pulled with a steady rhythm. Kham Ngai saw a cat pressed belly down against the earth, staring at a tree sparrow pecking at insects. The cat was inching forward stealthily, freezing whenever the bird looked up.

The heavy log dug up earth, the drag chain forming a perfectly straight line. Suddenly there was the crack of splitting wood. The nose holes had ripped and the chains snapped forward to hit the earth with a metallic bounce. Phlai Sut lost his footing and plunged forward dangerously. Kham

Ngai jerked back and then fell forward, his head smashing against the elephant's domed forehead. He had to grab the neck rope to keep from slipping to the ground.

He moved his legs to grip more tightly. The elephant was very upset and stood flapping his ears rapidly, making a dull thwack every time they hit his head. Kham Ngai looked behind and directed Phlai Sut back to the log. He tied the chains to the noseholes at the other end of the log and they dragged it away.

'I let my mind wander and almost fell,' he said out loud. He had forgotten entirely about the cat. When he turned to look around, it wasn't there. Neither was the tree sparrow. One of them had had good luck but certainly not both of them. If the bird was lucky, the cat had pounced for nothing. But if the cat was lucky, the bird was already torn to shreds.

Kham Ngai pictured a bird that had been attacked and felt great pity. Life is like that. 'Like me,' he said softly, thinking of the time the log had crushed his foot.

But living with people was not like that – with people it was possible to choose to avoid a heavy burden. He thought of the many times he and his friends had carried heavy poles to build a house. The man in the middle was expected to use all of his strength, but he was in a position where he could easily shirk, leaving all the weight to the men at the ends. He could appear to be working hard when in fact he was doing nothing at all.

In the places where it is possible to hide there must be people like that. People who don't really carry their share of the weight but go to great trouble to look as if they are doing so, he thought. I have to drag logs out in the open, and I can clearly see that if I don't exert myself to the utmost the logs won't move. There is no way to work any less than that.

It was the same as carving the elephant, he thought. Everything was difficult, but there is no way to escape it. Finally I came to realise the truth – that my body was very small. Before that I had grandiose dreams with no limits. But when I finally reached my own limits, I came to know the nightmares that lay there, to know that there was no way to fit such big dreams into such a little body. I felt as if I was struggling through a very thick forest, so thick that I could not even crawl. And then I came across a crystal clear river and saw myself perfectly reflected, just as if I were standing face to face with myself.

But, of course, everybody has their own dreams. Everybody has a big wooden elephant in their heart, to think of as being beautiful however they like. If they don't actually pick up a hammer and chisel and take them to that block of wood, then the elephant in their heart will stay beautiful forever, beautiful without limits. They will never see a river so transparent that you can see yourself reflected with perfect clarity.

'The Phaw Liang was here,' Majan told Kham Ngai as he was getting down from the elephant under the tamarind tree.

'What did he want?'

'He came to see your elephant statue.'

'What did he say?'

'He didn't say anything. He brought some big city people along with him.'

The next morning in front of the carving shop Boon Ham told Kham Ngai, 'The Phaw Liang wants to talk to you. You should go to his house.'

When Kham Ngai returned, Boon Ham asked, 'What's going on?'

'My wooden elephant,' Kham Ngai said. 'He'll give me Phlai Sut in exchange for it.'

'But it's not finished yet,' Majan said after Kham Ngai had told her the whole story that afternoon.

'Finished or not, he wants it. I've already agreed.'

Phlai Sut was under the tamarind tree knocking dirt off of grass roots with a series of flicks of his trunk. When they were clean he would eat them. His ears were flapping and he rubbed one leg against the other. Kham Ngai remembered when he was a boy and he would often hide from his father by concealing himself behind the elephant's two front legs. Phlai Sut would cleverly position his trunk so as to cover those parts of the boy that the massive legs failed to hide.

'Why is he willing to trade Phlai Sut for the statue?' Majan asked, watching Phlai Sut chew grass.

'He wants to sell the statue to those city people. He can get a lot more for it than he could get for a real elephant.'

The next morning, very early, Boon Ham was waiting for him in front of the workshop. Before Kham Ngai had even gotten off the elephant, Boon Ham hurriedly told him, 'You've got to drag that block of teak today. The carvers are going to start working on it tomorrow.'

'Did you get more rollers or not?'

'Yes.'

'Where are they?'

'The workers are bringing them. They'll be here in a minute.'

'I'll go wait by the log.'

'All right. I'll be there in a while.'

Kham Ngai let the elephant loose along the bank and then climbed to the top of the teak log and looked at the river far below. He saw a school of tiny mud carp rise and spread out, their mouths lifted above the surface of the water. When they were frightened they would flip their tails and disappear with a splash, the white drops sparkling in the sun.

A kingfisher, perched on a dry branch at the water's edge, flew into the air and hovered over the fish. Its wings moved so rapidly that they were a blur as the bird hung perfectly stationary. And then, in a split second, it dived and hit the water with a loud splash. The smooth surface shattered and rose in white spray. The fish swatted their tails, flipping their bodies to disappear. The kingfisher emerged from the water and flew back to his perch, a mud carp in his beak. The bird shook his feathers, sending beads of water flying, and then tossed his beak to grasp the fish more firmly. Then he darted down to stand at the hole in the bank below the teak block on which Kham Ngai was standing.

In a nearby vegetable garden, he saw a cat hiding in the shadows, staring at the kingfisher without stop. A little further down the bank there was a dog, his ears perked and his eyes searching everywhere.

Kham Ngai sat on the block of teak, his legs dangling over the side, and waited for the workers to bring the rollers to support the log. He was intently peeling bark off the log just to keep his hands busy. The Phaw Liang, Kham Ngai thought, was going to take this block of wood and carve it into an elephant. The Phaw Liang loved teak. His large and spacious house was made entirely of teak, and all of his furniture was made of teak. The Phaw Liang was very proud of this, and especially proud of the one hundred large teak pillars supporting his house.

'It's the very finest wood in the forest, all gathered together right here,' he was fond of telling his friends from the city when they came visiting.

Kham Ngai thought about the block of wood that he was sitting on. Now it was indisputably wood, but as soon as it was carved into an elephant hardly anybody would ever think of it as wood again. Carving is an even stranger transformation than stuffing the carcasses of animals, he thought.

When stuffing animals, he would take the carcass of a bird and make it into a bird, make a monkey into a monkey, a barking deer into a barking deer. But it didn't have to be like that always. Maybe some day somebody would take the body of a duck and turn it into a chicken. Or turn a monkey into a langur. Or a barking deer into a wild dog. Nobody would see anything strange in that.

He leaned his head back to look at the thick, billowing clouds, unrolling and moving apart, spreading out gradually all the time. Their shapes were ever changing and breaking up into bits of fluff until after a while they were absorbed into the backdrop leaving only the indigo blue sky.

'Let's get going!' Boon Ham shouted from a

distance. He was walking at the head of five workers, each carrying a round pole on his shoulder. When they reached the teak log the workers arranged the poles in a row on the ground in front of it, burying one pole in the earth so that the log wouldn't sink. One man used a shovel to make a smooth ramp so that the log would slide easily onto the rollers.

Kham Ngai climbed onto the elephant's neck and waited for a worker to tie the chains to the nose holes. When the man signalled, Kham Ngai urged Phlai Sut forward. The elephant strained against the breast band until the chains were taut. There was a cracking sound, but the nose holes held and the log moved. The men behind were noisily cheering Phlai Sut to pull harder, but he moved the block only six feet before it stopped. He pulled again.

The block of teak sank into the earth, pinning the rollers which no longer helped the log to slide smoothly. Phlai Sut managed to jerk the log forward a bit at a time while the men laid rollers on the ground at intervals. As soon as the log had been moved forward the space of one roller, a worker would lift the roller over which the log had just passed and run to the front to lay it before the log.

When the log had moved the space of two rollers, the work crew started to cheer; the log could be moved from the place where it was stuck.

But the log stalled again and everybody ran around in circles looking for the sticking point. When they couldn't find it, the men started shouting for Phlai Sut to pull even harder.

The elephant leaned his body, his legs bending forward in short spiky steps, his great muscles trembling. His long tail curled back and up, and lumps of green dung spilled out to pile on the ground – but the log had not budged. Kham Ngai sat on the elephant's neck, lifting his head to study the ground before him. Then he turned back to look at the log. Phlai Sut had pulled so hard he was shaking, but the encouraging shouts from behind did not stop.

Kham Ngai kicked vigorously with his legs to urge the elephant forward. He knew the animal was tired and had been overworked. He looked back at the log time and time again. He could not help but think that it was going to be carved into an elephant like Phlai Sut.

'They want this log so they can carve it into you,' he said softly but distinctly, as if he were talking to the elephant, not just to himself. 'You're dragging yourself, Phlai Sut. Endure a bit longer. You're not doing anything but dragging your own carcass.'

He stopped moving his feet for a moment and felt Phlai Sut straining so hard that Kham Ngai could feel the great sheets of muscle trembling on the neck, could feel the trembling pass through every part of his own body. 'You're dragging your own carcass. We're pulling our own carcass. It's not anything else. Let's do it. Don't stop! Pull!'

Kham Ngai felt that he was part of the elephant and that the elephant was part of him. Nobody is separable from anybody else, he told himself. When Aae died, he had felt unbearably morose and disturbed. He had thought so much about Aae's death that he had become totally confused, his thoughts a jumble. Aae was part of him, he thought, and I am part of Aae. Majan, too. The three of us, there's no way to separate us. None of us enjoys alone or suffers alone.

Everybody affects everybody else. Every human being has invisible threads that bind him to others. I am not me. And he is not him. I live in him, and he lives in me.

All of us are born only once and die only once. What lies in between is life – and we have to go and search that out for ourselves.

Truly, life is receiving shares. If I work for the Phaw Liang I get a portion as wages, and dragging logs is my portion of the work that goes with the wages. All the shares should balance out whether sad or happy, hungry or full, heavy or light. But most people want their share of obligations to be lighter than it should be. And even then they try to avoid burdens, unwilling to receive the responsibilities that come with the rewards.

Kham Ngai thought back to when he was floating rafts. Then he hadn't been dragging carcasses; he actually rode them – gliding rapidly downstream alongside the flooded banks. He was taking dead trees to the sawmill and then going home. It seemed that for his whole life he had been taking care of carcasses.

He recalled the price of a wooden elephant and thought, as if talking to Phlai Sut, take good care of the carcass. Take it to where it's going and make sure that it is not damaged – it is worth more than we are.

The raucous yells of the workers came from behind.

Phlai Sut lunged forward, smashing against his breast band, straining with all his power. He slammed against the harness again and then trumpeted. Kham Ngai was startled and then frightened. He looked behind and saw the workers prodding the elephant's hindquarters with wooden spears tipped with metal. He screamed, 'Stop!' but it did no good. The log jolted forward, careening crazily. Kham Ngai struggled to keep his balance.

The elephant laid a foot down on the ground in front of him but immediately lifted it and started to back up, but only to meet the spears of the workers. So he lurched forward again. As soon as his foot struck the soil, he jerked and then backed up very quickly, trumpeting with fear.

Kham Ngai yelled for the workers to stop, but nobody responded. It was as if they were very far away and could not hear. Kham Ngai tried to control the elephant, but the animal was trapped between fear and pain, trying to escape the terror behind.

The soil before them was very loose and crumbly. As soon as the elephant had stepped forward he had sensed that the ground would not bear his weight. He had backed up as quickly as he could. Kham Ngai knew and understood this instinct, so he once again shouted at the workers to stop.

But it made no difference. Phlai Sut strained against the breast band time after time, roaring with fear. The log shifted and rolled sideways. The surface of the earth broke and the log slid toward the edge of the bank. Phlai Sut fought to hold it, struggling so hard that his spine arched and his forehead touched the ground. He slid flat-footed across the soil, which was breaking up into chunks under his feet.

The sound of the earth caving in and the sound of the ground shaking merged with the faint sound of a drum. Kham Ngai thought indistinctly that he had heard that sound before, but the feeling quickly vanished.

There was nothing worth saving any more. The elephant was doing his best. He was on his own now. Nobody could help him. He would have to face everything by himself.

Phlai Sut used his trunk to grasp a tree the size of his leg. His mouth was dripping saliva and his eyes glistened. The long, tough muscles were coiled tightly, but the massive body began to lose its footing. When the edge of the bank collapsed, the tree roots were torn from the ground.

As the log caught at the edge of the bank and then teetered, there was no time to change anything. To beseech or to deny was useless. There was no time for anything, not even for fear.

It was a moment of truth in Kham Ngai's life. And it was happening in broad daylight where there were no shadows or crevices in which to hide. It was pure and clean. There was no good and no bad, no right or wrong. In the space of a single breath many things Kham Ngai had experienced in his life appeared. For that instant there was no time and there was no space. Everything melted together, blending harmoniously in expanding yellow petals blooming continually. There were yellow blossoms over the tree until it was all glowing. Yellow blossoms filled Kham Ngai's eyes and he instantly knew that the time of the flowering was not too short. It was just right.

The log tumbled over the bank, pulling Phlai Sut

behind it. The elephant's body slipped ever faster and then toppled over. Kham Ngai was lifted from Phlai Sut's neck and fell in the same rhythm as the elephant and the log. Clouds of red dust swirled around them like dense flocks of birds.

The tumbling log smashed down on Kham Ngai. The chains still did not break. The log jerked the elephant's body down on top of it, and then the elephant pulled the log back to it. They rolled over and over each other, careering through a garden and squashing the fresh green vegetables flat to the ground. A kingfisher darted into the air, as a dog and a cat scrambled in mad confusion through a curtain of red dust.

The day was very still and quiet, leaving the thick cloud of dust to float in the air for a long time before it gradually settled on the beach below. As the dust drifted down from the bank in a long trail, the picture gradually cleared.

On the gravel bed at the base of the bank, the elephant and the man and the log lay still in the glaring sun. The workers looking down stood dumbfounded.

Phlai Sut's body was disposed of immediately after Kham Ngai's cremation. The following day a big hauling truck and a hoist truck sped along kicking up dust until they came to a stop under the tamarind tree in front of Kham Ngai's house. Several men got down, and one muttered a few words to Majan while the trucks backed up to the door of the shed. The men folded the panels over to one side, and one man lifted a basket off the wooden elephant's trunk.

'What's this for?' he said and tossed the basket in a corner.

The men ripped off the grass roof and then ran a sling under the elephant's belly. It was quickly and easily hoisted up onto the truck and set on a cushion of soft jute sacks. Before Majan could even open her mouth to speak the two trucks drove out of the village, trailing long clouds of dust before disappearing across the open field.

The driver turned to the man sitting next to him and said, 'It was a stroke of luck that the Phaw Liang had already made the trade.'

In the morning there was fog. Majan carried a basket in one hand and with her other hand helped the little boy down the stairs. He was very happy and excited, full of life. The two of them walked through the wet grass to the top of the knoll and slipped into the fog. Above their heads was a soft rainbow. The gentle morning light began to warm the air.

Gaur   A large species of wild ox (*Bibos gaurus*) of Southeast Asia.

Hook   Ankus; the prod or goad which a mahout uses to control an elephant. A skilful mahout working with a well-trained elephant rarely uses the hook but rather depends on a combination of subtle body movements and about forty voice commands.

Langur   A long-tailed monkey, especially of the genus *Presbytis*, of Southeast Asia.

Mahout   An elephant driver.

Musth   A periodic condition, normally once a year, of male Asian elephants analogous to rut. Besides most often showing heightened sexual activity, elephants which 'go musth' are often violent and unpredictable, and are thus kept chained for a period of days, weeks, or months. Musth is characterised by a sticky and smelly secretion from the temporal glands, the external orifices of which are set halfway between the eyes and the ears on the elephant's temples.

Phaw Liang A local businessman with great influence, both financially and socially, in the north of Thailand. In central Thai the words 'Phaw Liang' simply mean 'Stepfather', but in northern Thai they might be best translated as 'Godfather', though without the criminal associations of that term, since a Phaw Liang is normally beneficent. A Phaw Liang might be considered the equivalent of a 'Patron' in many southern European countries.